SO-AYR-673

PAPERBACK TRADER
522 STORRS ROAD
PO BOX 677
MANSFIELD CENTER, CT 06250
(860)-456-0252

Edwards-Knox School Library
Russell, New York

A Haunt
of Ghosts

BOOKS BY AIDAN CHAMBERS

Dance On My Grave
Breaktime
The Present Takers
Seal Secret
Out of Time
Shades of Dark
Booktalk

014762

A Haunt of Ghosts

Stories by
Aidan Chambers
& Others

———— HARPER & ROW, PUBLISHERS ————

Cambridge, Philadelphia, San Francisco, Washington, London, Mexico City, São Paolo, Singapore, Sydney

———— NEW YORK ————

Edwards-Knox School Library
Russell, New York

SC
Hau

A Haunt of Ghosts
Copyright © 1987 by Aidan Chambers

All rights reserved. No part of this book may be used or reproduced in any manner whatsoever without written permission except in the case of brief quotations embodied in critical articles and reviews. Printed in the United States of America. For information address Harper & Row Junior Books, 10 East 53rd Street, New York, N.Y. 10022. Published simultaneously in Canada by Fitzhenry & Whiteside Limited, Toronto.
Typography by Joyce Hopkins
1 2 3 4 5 6 7 8 9 10
First Edition

Grateful acknowledgment is made as follows for the copyrighted material reprinted in this collection:
Joan Aiken for "Old Fillikin," © 1982 by Joan Aiken Enterprises Ltd; John Gordon for "If She Bends, She Breaks," © 1982 by John Gordon; Jan Mark and her agent, Murray Pollinger, for "Absalom, Absalom," © 1982 by Jan Mark; Lance Salway and Lutterworth Press for "Such a Sweet Little Girl," © 1982 by Lance Salway; all of which first appeared in *Ghost After Ghost*, compiled by Aidan Chambers, published by Kestrel Books, © 1982 by Aidan Chambers.
Aidan Chambers's stories first appeared as follows:
"Room 18" in *Ghosts*, compiled by Aidan and Nancy Chambers, published by Macmillan (London), © 1969 by Malcolm Blacklin. "Dead Trouble," "Last Respects," "Nancy Tucker's Ghost" and "Seeing Is Believing" in *Ghosts 2*, by Aidan Chambers, published by Macmillan (London), © 1972 by Aidan Chambers.
"The Haunted and the Haunters, or the House and the Brain," by Edward Bulwer-Lytton, edited and abridged by Aidan Chambers, © 1969 by Aidan Chambers.

Library of Congress Cataloging-in-Publication Data
A haunt of ghosts.

"A Charlotte Zolotow book."
Summary: A collection of ten ghost stories by authors including Aidan Chambers, Joan Aiken, and Edward Bulwer-Lytton.
1. Ghost stories, English. [1. Ghosts—Fiction. 2. Short stories] I. Chambers, Aidan.
PZ5.H27 1987 [Fic] 86-45486
ISBN 0-06-021206-3
ISBN 0-06-021207-1 (lib. bdg.)

8/09

Contents

Foreword   ix

Such a Sweet Little Girl   *Lance Salway*   3

Last Respects   *Aidan Chambers*   19

If She Bends, She Breaks   *John Gordon*   27

Seeing Is Believing   *Aidan Chambers*   46

Absalom, Absalom   *Jan Mark*   72

Room 18   *Aidan Chambers*   91

Old Fillikin   *Joan Aiken*   106

Dead Trouble   *Aidan Chambers*   119

Nancy Tucker's Ghost   *Aidan Chambers*   142

The Haunted and the Haunters   *Edward Bulwer-Lytton*   154

Foreword

This gathering of ghosts includes five of my own stories mingled with four by some of my favorite living authors, and one which I think is probably the greatest ghost story ever written.

What I like so much about Edward Bulwer-Lytton's "The Haunted and the Haunters" is that it contains all the ingredients I most enjoy in ghost stories: a mystery, plenty of suspense, a spooky atmosphere right from the beginning, intriguing and sometimes nerve-tingling details, and a convincing yet elusive specter. In fact, it was based on a true event. More than a hundred years ago a large house in Berkeley Square, London, was the scene of a terrifying and now famous haunting. The house was supposed to be inhabited by a shapeless apparition, the mere sight of which led to the victim's death. As a result, the building stood empty for many years.

Edward Bulwer-Lytton's fictional version of that story

was written in elaborate, old-fashioned language which I have edited slightly so as to make it more suitable for our taste today. And I have placed it at the end of the book as a kind of grand finale.

Like "The Haunted and the Haunters," many of my own stories are also based on real events. As the son of an undertaker, I had no difficulty at all imagining the ghost who appears in "Last Respects." "Seeing Is Believing" had its origin in a Scottish haunting and owes a debt in the way it is told to Edward Bulwer-Lytton's masterpiece. "Room 18" began when I heard from a friend about a hotel room that disappeared after a curious haunting took place in it. My friend did not know exactly what had happened, so I invented the details. And "Nancy Tucker's Ghost" is a very free retelling of a folk legend about a stagecoach driver who worked on the same route as one of my relatives did at the time the story takes place. Naturally, I like to think my great-great-grandfather is the driver who sees Nancy! The last of my stories, however, is pure invention. I wanted to write a story from the point of view of the ghost and to make it amusing. "Dead Trouble" was the result.

All the other stories were written at my request by writers whose work I admire. Lance Salway's "Such a Sweet Little Girl" is a frighteningly sinister tale. John Gordon's "If She Bends, She Breaks" involves a chillingly believable ghost made of ice. The misadventure that befalls Jan Mark's unfortunate hero in "Absalom, Absalom" warns of the dangers of vanity and long hair. I was never the slightest use at math when I was at school, so I sympathize with Timothy in Joan Aiken's "Old Fillikin" and enjoy the strange consequences that result from the help his grandmother gives him. Which says enough, I hope, to show you that each of my companions' stories is different from the others. And in my opinion each is brilliantly successful of its kind. I hope you enjoy them as much as I do.

AIDAN CHAMBERS

A Haunt
of Ghosts

Lance Salway

Such a Sweet Little Girl

It was at breakfast on a bright Saturday morning that Julie first made her announcement. She put down her spoon, swallowed a last mouthful of cornflakes, and said, "There's a ghost in my bedroom."

No one took any notice. Her mother was writing a shopping list and her father was deep in his newspaper. Neither of them heard what she said. Her brother Edward heard but he ignored her, which is what he usually did. Edward liked to pretend that Julie didn't exist. It wasn't easy but he did his best.

Julie tried again. She raised her voice and said, "There's a ghost in my bedroom."

Mrs. Bennett looked up from her list. "Is there, dear? Oh, good. Do you think we need more marmalade? And I suppose I'd better buy a cake or something if your friends are coming to tea."

Edward said sharply, "Friends? What friends?"

"Sally and Rachel are coming to tea with Julie this afternoon," his mother said.

Edward gave a loud theatrical groan. "Oh, no. Why does she have to fill the house with her rotten friends?"

"You could fill the house with *your* friends, too," Julie said sweetly. "If you had any."

Edward looked at her with loathing. "Oh, I've got friends all right," he said. "I just don't inflict them on other people."

"You haven't got any friends," Julie said quietly. "You haven't got any friends because no one likes you."

"That's enough," Mr. Bennett said, looking up from his paper, and there was silence then, broken only by the gentle rumble-slush, rumble-slush of the washing machine in the corner.

Edward chewed a piece of toast and thought how much he hated Julie. He hated a lot of people. Most people, in fact. But there were some he hated more than others. Mr. Jenkins, who taught math. And that woman in the paper shop who'd accused him of stealing chewing gum, when everyone knew he never touched the stuff. And Julie. He hated Julie most of all. He hated her pretty pale face and her pretty fair curls and her pretty little lisping voice. He hated the grown-ups who constantly fluttered round her, saying how enchanting she was, and so clever for her age, and wasn't Mrs. Bennett lucky to have such a sweet little girl. What they didn't say, but he knew they were thinking it behind their wide bright smiles, was poor Mrs. Bennett, with that lumpy, sullen boy. So different from his sister. So different from lovely little Julie.

Lovely little Julie flung her spoon on the table. "I *said* there's a ghost in my bedroom."

Mrs. Bennett put down her shopping list and ballpoint in order to give Julie her full attention. "Oh dear," she said. "I hope it didn't frighten you, darling."

Julie smiled and preened. "No," she said smugly. "*I* wasn't frightened."

Edward tried to shut his ears. He knew this dialogue by heart. The Bennett family spent a great deal of time adjusting their habits to suit Julie's fantasies. Once, for a whole month, they had all been forced to jump the bottom tread of the staircase because Julie insisted that two invisible rabbits were sleeping there. For a time she had been convinced, or so she said, that a pink dragon lived in the airing cupboard. And there had been a terrible few weeks the year before when all communication with her had to be conducted through an invisible fairy called Priscilla who lived on her left shoulder.

And now there was a ghost in her bedroom.

Try as he might, Edward couldn't shut out his sister's voice. On and on it whined: ". . . I was really very brave and didn't run away even though it was so frightening, and I said . . ."

Edward looked at his parents with contempt. His father had put down the newspaper and was gazing at Julie with a soppy smile on his face. His mother was wearing the mock-serious expression that adults often adopt in order to humor their young. Edward hated them for it. If he'd told them a story about a ghost when *he* was seven, they'd have told him to stop being so silly, there's no such thing

5

as ghosts, why don't you grow up, be a man.

"What sort of ghost is it?" he asked suddenly.

Julie looked at him in surprise. Then her eyes narrowed. "It's a frightening ghost," she said. "With great big eyes and teeth and horrible, nasty claws. Big claws. And it smells."

"Ghosts aren't like that," Edward said scornfully. "Ghosts have clanking chains and skeletons, and they carry their heads under their arms."

"This ghost doesn't," Julie snapped.

"Funny sort of ghost, then."

"You don't know anything about it."

Julie's voice was beginning to tremble. Edward sighed. There'd be tears soon and he'd get the blame. As usual.

"Come now, Edward," his father said heartily. "It's only pretend. Isn't it, lovey?"

Lovey shot him a vicious glance. "It's *not* pretend. It's a real ghost. And it's in my bedroom."

"Of course, darling," Mrs. Bennett picked up her shopping list again. "How are we off for chutney, I wonder?"

But Edward wasn't going to let the matter drop. Not this time. "Anyway," he said, "ghosts don't have claws."

"This one does," Julie said.

"Then you're lying."

"I'm not. There *is* a ghost. I saw it."

"Liar."

"I'm not!" She was screaming now. "I'll show you I'm not. I'll tell it to *get* you. With its claws. It'll come and get you with its claws."

"Don't make me laugh."

"*Edward!* That's *enough!*" His mother stood up and started to clear the table. "Don't argue."

"But there isn't a ghost," Edward protested. "There can't be!"

Mrs. Bennett glanced uneasily at Julie. "Of course there is," she said primly. "If Julie says so."

"She's a liar, a nasty little liar."

Julie kicked him hard, then, under the table. Edward yelped, and kicked back. Julie let out a screech, and then her face crumpled and she began to wail.

"*Now* look what you've done," Mrs. Bennett snapped. "Oh *really*, Edward. You're twice her age. Why can't you leave her alone?"

"Because she's a liar, that's why." Edward stood up and pushed his chair aside. "Because there isn't a ghost in her bedroom. And even if there is, it won't have claws." And he turned, and stormed out of the kitchen.

He came to a stop in the sitting room, and crossed over to the window to see what sort of day it was going to be. Sunny, by the look of it. A small tightly cropped lawn lay in front of the house, a lawn that was identical in size and appearance to those in front of the other identical square brick houses which lined the road. Edward laughed out loud. Any ghost worthy of the name would wither away from boredom in such surroundings. No, there weren't any ghosts in Briarfield Gardens. With or without heads under their arms. With or without claws.

He turned away from the window. The day had started badly, thanks to Julie. And it would continue badly, thanks to Julie and her rotten friends who were coming to tea.

And there was nothing he could do about it. Or was there? On the coffee table by the television set there lay a half-finished jigsaw puzzle. Julie had been working on it for ages, her fair curls bent earnestly over the table day after day. According to the picture on the box, the finished puzzle would reveal a thatched cottage surrounded by a flower-filled garden. When it was finished. If.

Edward walked across to the table and smashed the puzzle with one quick, practiced movement of his hand. Pieces fell and flew and scattered on the carpet in a storm of colored cardboard. And then he turned, and ran upstairs to his room.

He hadn't long to wait. After a few minutes he heard the sounds that he was expecting. The kitchen door opening. A pause. Then a shrill, furious shriek, followed by loud sobbing. Running footsteps. A quieter comforting voice. Angry footsteps on the stairs. The rattling of the handle on his locked bedroom door. And then Julie's voice, not like a seven-year-old voice at all anymore but harsh and bitter with hate.

"The ghost'll get you, Edward. I'm going to tell it to get you. With its claws. With its sharp, horrible claws."

And then, quite suddenly, Edward felt afraid.

The fear didn't last long. It had certainly gone by lunchtime, when Edward was given a ticking-off by his father for upsetting dear little Julie. And by the time Julie's friends arrived at four, he was quite his old self again.

"The ugly sisters are here!" he announced loudly as he opened the front door, having beaten Julie to it by a short head.

8

She glared at him, and quickly hustled Sally and Rachel up the stairs to her room.

Edward felt a bit guilty. Sally and Rachel weren't at all ugly. In fact, he quite liked them both. He ambled into the kitchen, where his mother was busy preparing tea.

She looked up when he came in. "I do hope you're going to behave yourself this evening," she said. "We don't want a repetition of this morning's little episode, do we?"

"Well, she asked for it," Edward said sullenly, and sneaked a biscuit from a pile on a plate.

"Hands off!" his mother said automatically. "Julie did *not* ask for it. She was only pretending. You know what she's like. There was no need for you to be so nasty. And there was certainly no excuse for you to break up her jigsaw puzzle like that."

Edward shuffled uneasily and stared at the floor.

"She *is* only seven, after all," Mrs. Bennett went on, slapping chocolate icing on a sponge cake as she did so. "You must make allowances. The rest of us do."

"She gets away with murder," Edward mumbled. "Just because she's such a sweet little girl."

"Nonsense!" his mother said firmly. "And keep your mucky paws off those ginger snaps. If anyone gets away with murder in this house, it's you."

"But she can't really expect us to believe there's a ghost in her bedroom," Edward said. "Do *you* believe her? Come on, mum, do you?"

"I—" his mother began, and then she was interrupted by a familiar lisping voice.

"You *do* believe me, Mummy, don't you?"

Julie was standing at the kitchen door. Edward wondered how long she'd been there. And how much she'd heard.

"Of course I do, darling," Mrs. Bennett said quickly. "Now run along, both of you. Or I'll never have tea ready in time."

Julie stared at Edward for a moment with her cold blue eyes, and then she went out of the kitchen as quietly as she'd entered it.

Tea passed off smoothly enough. Julie seemed to be on her best behavior, but that was probably because her friends were there and she wanted to create a good impression. Edward followed her example. Julie didn't look at him or speak to him, but there was nothing unusual about that. She and the others chattered brightly about nothing in particular, and Edward said nothing at all.

It was dusk by the time they'd finished tea and it was then that Julie suggested that they all play ghosts. She looked straight at Edward when she said this, and the proposal seemed like a challenge.

"Can anyone play?" he asked. "Or is it just a game for horrible little girls?"

"Edward!" warned his mother.

"Of course you can play, Edward," said Julie. "You *must* play."

"But not in the kitchen or in the dining room," said Mrs. Bennett. "And keep out of our bedroom. I'll go and draw all the curtains and make sure the lights are switched off."

"All right," said Julie, and the other little girls clapped their hands with excitement.

"How do we play this stupid game?" said Edward.

"Oh, it's easy," said Julie. "One of us is the ghost, and she has to frighten the others. If the ghost catches you and scares you, you have to scream and drop down on the floor. As if you were dead."

"Like 'Murder in the Dark'?" asked Sally.

"Yes," said Julie. "Only we don't have a detective or anything like that."

"It sounds like a crummy game to me," said Edward. "I don't think I'll play."

"Oh, *do!*" chorused Sally and Rachel. "Please!"

And Julie came up to him and whispered, "You must play, Edward. And don't forget what I said this morning. About my ghost. And how it's going to get you with its claws."

"You must be joking!" Edward jeered. "And, anyway, I told you. Ghosts don't have claws." He looked her straight in the eyes. "Of course I'll play."

Julie smiled, and then turned to the others and said, "I'll be the ghost to start with. The rest of you run and hide. I'll count up to fifty and then I'll come and haunt you."

Sally and Rachel galloped upstairs, squealing with excitement. Edward wandered into the hall and stood for a moment, wondering where to hide. It wasn't going to be easy. Their small brick box of a house didn't offer many possibilities. After a while he decided on the sitting room. It was the most obvious place and Julie would never think of looking there. He opened the door quietly, ducked down behind an armchair, and waited.

Silence settled over the house. Apart from washing-up

sounds from the kitchen, all was quiet. Edward made himself comfortable on the carpet and waited for the distant screams that would tell him that Sally had been discovered, or Rachel. But no sounds came. As he waited, ears straining against the silence, the room grew darker. The day was fading and it would soon be night.

And then, suddenly, Edward heard a slight noise near the door. His heart leaped and, for some reason, his mouth went dry. And then the fear returned, the unaccountable fear he had felt that morning when Julie hissed her threat through his bedroom door.

The air seemed much colder now, but that could only be his imagination, surely. But he knew that he wasn't imagining the wild thumping of his heart or the sickening lurching of his stomach. He remembered Julie's words and swallowed hard.

"The ghost'll get you, Edward. With its claws. With its sharp, horrible claws."

He heard sounds again, closer this time. A scuffle. Whispering. Or was it whispering? Someone was there. Something. He tried to speak, but gave only a curious croak. And then, "Julie?" he said. "I know you're there. I know it's you."

Silence. A dark terrible silence. And then the light snapped on and the room was filled with laughter and shouts of "Got you! Caught you! The ghost has caught you!" and he saw Julie's face alive with triumph and delight, and, behind her, Sally and Rachel grinning, and the fear was replaced by an anger far darker and more intense than the terror he'd felt before.

"Edward's scared of the ghost!" Julie jeered. "Edward's

a scaredy-cat! He's frightened! He's frightened of the gho-ost!"

And Rachel and Sally echoed her. "He's frightened! He's frightened of the gho-ost!"

"I'm not!" Edward shouted. "I'm not scared! There isn't a ghost!" And he pushed past Julie and ran out of the room and up the stairs. He'd show her. He'd prove she didn't have a ghost. There were no such things as ghosts. She didn't have a ghost in her room. She didn't.

Julie's bedroom was empty. Apart from the furniture and the pictures and the toys and dolls and knick-knacks. He opened the wardrobe and pulled shoes and games out on to the floor. He burrowed in drawers, scattering books and stuffed animals and clothes around him. At last he stopped, gasping for breath. And turned.

His mother was standing in the doorway, staring at him in amazement. Clustered behind her were the puzzled, anxious faces of Sally and Rachel. And behind them, Julie. Looking at him with her ice-blue eyes.

"What on earth are you doing?" his mother asked.

"See?" he panted. "There isn't a ghost here. She hasn't got a ghost in her bedroom. There's nothing here. Nothing."

"Isn't there?" said Julie. "Are you sure you've looked properly?"

Sally—or was it Rachel?—gave a nervous giggle.

"That's enough," said Mrs. Bennett. "Now I suggest you tidy up the mess you've made in here, Edward, and then go to your room. I don't know why you're behaving so strangely. But it's got to stop. It's got to."

She turned and went downstairs. Sally and Rachel fol-

13

lowed her. Julie lingered by the door, and stared mockingly at Edward. He stared back.

"It's still here, you know," she said at last. "The ghost is still here. And it'll get you."

"You're a dirty little liar!" he shouted. "A nasty, filthy little liar!"

Julie gaped at him for a moment, taken aback by the force of his rage. Then, "It'll get you!" she screamed. "With its claws. Its horrible claws. It'll get you tonight. When you're asleep. Because I hate you. I hate you. Yes, it'll *really* get you. Tonight."

It was dark when Edward awoke. At first he didn't know where he was. And then he remembered. He was in bed. In his bedroom. It was the middle of the night. And he remembered, too, Julie's twisted face and the things she said. The face and the words had kept him awake, and had haunted his dreams when at last he slept.

It was ridiculous, really. All this fuss about an imaginary ghost. Why did he get in such a state over Julie? She was only a little kid, after all. His baby sister. You were supposed to love your sister, not—not fear her. But no, he wasn't *really* afraid of her. How could he be? Such a sweet little girl with blue eyes and fair bouncing curls who was half his age. A little girl who played games and imagined things. Who imagined ghosts. A ghost in her bedroom.

But he *was* frightened. He knew that now. And as his fear mounted again, the room seemed to get colder. He shut his eyes and snuggled down under the blankets, shutting out the room and the cold. But not the fear.

14

And then he heard it. A sound. A faint scraping sound, as though something heavy was being dragged along the landing. A sound that came closer and grew louder. A wet, slithering sound. And with it came a smell, a sickening smell of, oh, drains and dead leaves and decay. And the sound grew louder and he could hear breathing, harsh breathing, long choking breaths coming closer.

"Julie?" Edward said, and then he repeated it, louder. "Julie!"

But there was no answer. All he heard was the scraping, dragging sound coming closer, closer. Near his door now. Closer.

"I know it's you!" Edward shouted, and heard the fear in his voice. "You're playing ghosts again, aren't you? Aren't you?"

And then there was silence. No sound at all. Edward sat up in bed and listened. The awful slithering noise had stopped. It had gone. The ghost had gone.

He hugged himself with relief. It had been a dream, that's all. He'd imagined it. Just as Julie imagined things. Imagined ghosts.

Then he heard the breathing again. The shuddering, choking breaths. And he knew that the thing hadn't gone. That it was still there. Outside his door. Waiting. Waiting.

And Edward screamed, "Julie! Stop it! Stop it! Please stop it! I believe you! I believe in the ghost!"

The door opened. The shuddering breaths seemed to fill the room, and the smell, and the slithering wet sound of a shape, something, coming towards him, something huge and dark and—

15

And he screamed as the claws, yes, the claws tore at his hands, his chest, his face. And he screamed again as the darkness folded over him.

When Julie woke up and came downstairs, the ambulance had gone. Her mother was sitting alone in the kitchen, looking pale and frightened. She smiled weakly when she saw Julie, and then frowned.

"Darling," she said. "I did so hope you wouldn't wake up. I didn't want you to be frightened—"

"What's the matter, Mummy?" said Julie. "Why are you crying?"

Her mother smiled again, and drew Julie to her, folding her arms around her so that she was warm and safe. "You must be very brave, darling," she said. "Poor Edward has been hurt. We don't know what happened but he's been very badly hurt."

"Hurt? What do you mean, Mummy?"

Her mother brushed a stray curl from the little girl's face. "We don't know what happened, exactly. Something attacked him. His face—" Her voice broke then, and she looked away quickly. "He has been very badly scratched. They're not sure if his eyes—" She stopped and fumbled in her dressing-gown pocket for a tissue.

"I expect my ghost did it," Julie said smugly.

"What did you say, dear?"

Julie looked up at her mother. "My ghost did it. I told it to. I told it to hurt Edward because I hate him. The ghost hurt him. The ghost in my bedroom."

Mrs. Bennett stared at Julie. "This is no time for games,"

she said. "We're very upset. Your father's gone to the hospital with Edward. We don't know if—" Her eyes filled with tears. "I'm in no mood for your silly stories about ghosts, Julie. Not now. I'm too upset."

"But it's true!" Julie said. "My ghost *did* do it. Because I told it to."

Mrs. Bennett pushed her away and stood up. "All right, Julie, that's enough. Back to bed now. You can play your game tomorrow."

"But it's not a game," Julie persisted. "It's true! My ghost—"

And then she saw the angry expression on her mother's face, and she stopped. Instead, she snuggled up to her and whispered, "I'm sorry, Mummy. You're right. I *was* pretending. I was only pretending about the ghost. There isn't a ghost in my room. I was making it all up. And I'm so sorry about poor Edward."

Mrs. Bennett relaxed and smiled and drew Julie to her once more. "That's my baby," she said softly. "That's my sweet little girl. Of course you were only pretending. Of course there wasn't a ghost. Would I let a nasty ghost come and frighten my little girl? Would I? Would I?"

"No, Mummy," said Julie. "Of course you wouldn't."

"Off you go to bed now."

"Good night, Mummy," said Julie.

"Sleep well, my pet," said her mother.

And Julie walked out of the kitchen and into the hall and up the stairs to her bedroom. She went inside and closed the door behind her.

And the ghost came out to meet her.

17

"She doesn't believe me, either," Julie said. "She doesn't believe me. We'll have to show her, won't we? Just as we showed Edward."

And the ghost smiled and nodded, and they sat down together, Julie and the ghost, and decided what they would do.

Aidan Chambers

Last Respects

I suppose there aren't many people whose fathers were undertakers. There can't be when you think about it; there are only a few hundred undertakers in all Britain, not counting the jobbing joiners who do the odd funeral on the side. But, as I say, my father was an undertaker and that is why I have this story to tell.

I was fifteen at the time. Father had his own small business with premises in a street just off the main road into town. There was a chemist's shop on one side and a florist's on the other. Mother, father, and myself lived in the rooms above the offices, which fronted onto the street. There was a big window with a wide black border painted on it edged with gold and in the middle hung an illuminated sign with black and gold lettering that read:

GEORGE MIDDLETON
FUNERAL DIRECTOR
DAY AND NIGHT SERVICE

Inside the main door there was a hall, carpeted, and paneled in light oak. On one side of the hall was a room where Dad's secretary worked, dealing with customers who called to make arrangements for funerals or to pay their bills. On the other side was Dad's office. Then there was a door that led to the stairs up to our living-rooms; and in the wall facing the main entrance, double doors which opened into a back passage off which there was a carpenter's shop where coffins were prepared. Opposite the carpenter's shop was a Chapel of Rest. This was a room done up like a very small church. There was nothing in it but a little wooden altar and two trestles in the middle of the floor. Coffins were placed on the trestles, coffins with their lids off so that the bodies could be seen by relatives coming to pay their last respects to their dead.

I never much liked the Chapel of Rest. To start with, I don't go much on dead bodies lying around the place, their cold, waxen faces uncovered—it was something I never quite got used to. In the second place, the chapel was right under my bedroom, and you can imagine what I thought if ever there was an odd noise in the night!

Well, one evening Mother and Dad went off to the cinema, leaving me alone in the house. We always had to have someone available to take the names and addresses of new clients, and to attend to relatives who called to view a body after office hours. Naturally, if Mother and Dad went out for the evening, I was the one who had to stay in—a kind of body-sitter instead of a baby-sitter. I grumbled about having to do such a boring job, but, to be honest, Dad was very fair and paid me for the time I spent "on duty," so I earned extra pocket money for what was usually pretty easy work.

On this particular night, I watched TV for a while, then read until about ten-thirty. Things were quiet, not a phone call nor a visit by a client to keep me from getting bored. Finally, I decided to write a few letters (I was going through a pen-pal craze at the time). I looked in the living-room desk for some paper, but couldn't find any. So I went downstairs, thinking I would take some from the secretary's office.

I saw him as I pushed open the door leading into the hall—a man standing in the middle of the room, his back towards me. I jumped with fright, and stopped dead in my tracks. My thoughts had been far away, and as I had not heard the front door bell, I did not expect to see anyone in the building. There was no light on, either, which made matters worse, more startling; I only had the reflected light from the illuminated sign in the window to see by.

Recovering from the shock, I said, "Can I help you?"

The man seemed as startled by my presence as I had been at his. He swung round to face me. As he did so I switched on the hall lights.

He was tall, well-built, with grey hair, thinning on top, and wearing a neat blue suit. He looked a solid, respectable old man, with little about him that would have distinguished him in a crowd. He might have been a bank clerk or something of that sort. Only his eyebrows were unusual. They were very bushy, a hedge of hair that stretched unbroken across his forehead, throwing his eyes into deep shadow, and they turned up at the ends where long wispy hairs grew out like little horns. I'd never seen eyebrows quite like them before; I felt I wanted to grab a pair of scissors and trim them.

I said again—for he was staring at me now, speechless and motionless: "Can I help you?"

He looked at me quizzically. I was quite used to this response from clients. It meant: What is a lad like you doing here?

"I'm Mr. Middleton's son," I said. "My father is out at present. Is there anything I can do?"

He seemed reassured by this, and smiled.

"I wonder," he said hesitantly, as though searching for words. (This was nothing unusual either. Most people are nervous when they come to an undertaker's!) "I wonder . . . if I might see my . . . er . . . see Mr. Clayton. I believe . . . he is in your Chapel of Rest."

"Are you a relative?" I asked, politely but firmly. You'd never believe how careful you have to be. Some people are odd. There was an old woman round our way who loved looking at dead bodies. She was always trying to get into mortuaries so she could look at them. Anyway, Dad had warned me many times to let only genuine relatives and friends into the Chapel. Hence the cross-examination before admittance!

"Yes," the man said, smiling. "I'm a relative . . . a very close one . . . very close . . ."

He was a nice old guy; his voice was quiet and gentle, his manners impeccable. I was rather taken by him. Somehow it seemed rude to question him any further. He was obviously "genuine"!

"Would you come this way, then, please," I said, and walked to the double doors leading into the back passage. As I went through, I switched on the lights in the passage and in the Chapel of Rest. Then I went to the Chapel door, slid it open, and stood aside for him to enter.

When I looked round he was standing behind me, the same nervous smile on his face, the same strange motionless posture. When I think back now, I realize that I never actually saw the old man move except when he swung round to face me in the hall, and then the place was pretty dark, as I've said. Anyway, it strikes me as strange now.

I waited a second or two for him to go inside. But he just stood there in the passage, unmoving. Many people, I must explain, find viewing the body of a relative something of an ordeal. Some people like to do it accompanied by another person, even if only by the undertaker. It helps them keep calm. But others prefer to be alone, to cope with their grief unwatched. Undertakers get used to all kinds of behavior and look out for the signs that give away how each person will react, and then respond accordingly, without fuss or embarrassment. It is part of the job of being what my father calls "a good boxer"! I took this man's hesitancy to mean he wanted to be on his own.

"I'll leave you to pay your last respects alone," I said, "and come back in a few minutes."

"Thank you," he said in his quiet voice. "I am most grateful."

So I left him there and went into the hall and then into the secretary's office to get the writing paper I wanted.

23

Leaving the office door wide open so that I would be sure to see him if he came back into the hall, I sat at the secretary's desk and began writing my letter to pass the time until he had finished.

Five minutes went by without my hearing a sound or seeing the man return. Usually on these occasions people only take a few minutes, for no one cares to spend long at such a distressing business. Thinking that the old man couldn't be long now, I went into the hall ready to let him out of the building.

Another five minutes went by. My patience was beginning to fray.

Maybe, I thought, he has got lost in his thoughts and forgotten the time. I went to the double doors and coughed.

Still no response.

Then I started to worry. Maybe he had fainted! People very upset by death have been known to do so. My father carried a bottle of smelling salts in his pocket for that very reason.

I walked hurriedly to the Chapel door and looked inside.

The visitor wasn't there. Not a sign of him.

But where could he be? It was impossible for him to have got out without my knowing.

Nervously, I edged into the room. It was only a small place, no more than twelve feet by eight, and with nothing in it but the altar against the wall and the coffin on its trestles. There was nowhere to hide or faint away out of sight. The man just *had* to be here!

But he wasn't. As my eyes searched the room, I glanced at the body in the coffin. Even though I was standing at its head, looking, so to speak, at the face upside down, one feature sprang out at me. The eyebrows.

The corpse had the same grey, bushy line of hair unbroken across his forehead, and at each end grew the same wispy little horns.

Letting out an incredulous "No!" I stepped forward so that I could look squarely into the waxen face.

I was not mistaken. The eyebrows were the same. So too was every other detail of the features: the grey hair, thinning on top, the same shape of head, the same nose and mouth and set of the jaw. I could not have told the living man from the dead.

Chills ran down my spine; my flesh came out in a rash of goose-pimples.

Then a saving thought burrowed its way through the shock in my brain. A close relative, the man had said—very close. How close? Close enough to be an identical twin?

I rushed from the Chapel, back into the secretary's office. In a fever of haste I riffled through her records of cases currently being attended to.

Clayton . . . Clayton . . .

Clayton, John Howard

Age: 64

Address . . . Date of death . . .

"Next of kin," I read aloud, reaching the column at last. And paused, catching my breath.

Next of kin: None.

"But . . ." I stammered.

Another thought: Who is arranging for the funeral?

Client: Hayes and Bottomley, Solicitors

I sat down heavily in the secretary's swivel chair.

Was it possible? Could the man who came to pay his last respects be . . . ?

Never! It was too frightening, too unbelievable to think so.

For the first time since I had been surprised by the figure standing in the dark hall, I thought of the main door. When they left me alone in the house, Mother and Dad always locked the door behind them. How then had the man got in? Pushing myself to my feet, I ran to the front door.

Sure enough, the Yale was firmly fastened.

That was enough for me. Leaving the lights blazing, I fled to the secure familiarity of our living-room, and refused to stir from it until my parents returned home.

Dad, of course, would not believe my story, hardened sceptic that he is. Mother said nothing. But I have never doubted for a moment that the man who came to pay his last respects to the body of John Howard Clayton, lying unvisited by relative or friend in our Chapel of Rest, was no other than Mr. John Howard Clayton's departing spirit.

John Gordon

If She Bends, She Breaks

Ben had felt strange ever since the snow started falling. He looked out of the classroom window and saw that it had come again, sweeping across like a curtain. That was exactly what it seemed to be: a curtain. The snow had come down like a blank sheet in his mind, and he could remember nothing beyond it. He could not even remember getting up this morning or walking to school; yesterday was only a haze, and last week did not exist. And now, at this moment, he did not know whether it was morning or afternoon. He began to get to his feet, but dizziness made him sit down.

"I know it's been freezing hard." Miss Carter's voice from the front of the class seemed distant. He wanted to tell her he felt unwell, but just for the moment he did not have the energy. She had her back to the stove as usual, and the eyes behind her glasses stared like a frightened horse's as they always did when she was in a passion. "It's been freezing hard," she repeated, "but the ice is still far too dangerous, and nobody is to go anywhere near it. Do you understand?"

Tommy Drake, in the next desk to Ben, murmured something and grinned at somebody on Ben's other side. But he ignored Ben completely.

"Tommy Drake!" Miss Carter had missed nothing. "What did you say?"

"Nothing, miss."

"Then why are you grinning like a jackass? If there's a joke, we all want to hear it. On your feet."

As Tommy pushed back in his chair, Ben smiled at him weakly, but Tommy seemed to be in no mood for him and winked at somebody else as though Ben himself was not there.

"Well?" Miss Carter was waiting.

Tommy stood in silence.

"Very well. If you are not going to share your thoughts with the rest of us, perhaps you will remind me of what I was saying a moment ago."

"About the ice, miss?"

"And what about the ice?"

"That it's dangerous, miss." Then Tommy, who did not lack courage, went on, "What I was saying was that you can always tell if it's safe."

"Oh you can, can you?" Miss Carter pursed her lips, and again waited.

"If she cracks, she bears," said Tommy. "If she bends, she breaks." It was a lesson they all knew in the flat fenland where everybody skated in winter. A solid cracking sound in the ice was better than a soft bending. But it meant nothing to Miss Carter.

"Stuff and nonsense!" she cried.

"But everybody know it's true." Tommy had justice on his side and his round face was getting red.

"Old wives' tales!" Miss Carter was not going to listen to reason. "Sit down."

Ben saw that Tommy was going to argue, and the sudden urge to back him up made him forget his dizziness. He got to his feet. "It's quite true, miss," he said. "I've tried it out."

She paid no attention to him. She glared at Tommy. "Sit down!"

Tommy obeyed, and Miss Carter pulled her cardigan tighter over her dumpy figure.

"Listen to me, all of you." Her voice was shrill. "I don't care what anybody says in the village; I won't have any of you go anywhere near that ice. Do you hear? Nobody!" She paused, and then added softly, "You all know what can happen."

She had succeeded in silencing the classroom and, as she turned away to her own desk, she muttered something to the front row, who began putting their books away. It was time for break.

Ben was still standing. In her passion she seemed not to have seen him. "What's up with her?" he said, but Tommy was on his feet and heading towards the cloakroom with the rest.

The dizziness came over Ben again. Could nobody see that he was unwell? Or was his illness something so terrible

29

that everybody wanted to ignore it? The classroom had emptied, and Miss Carter was wiping her nose on a crumpled paper handkerchief. He would tell her how he felt, and perhaps she would get his sister to walk home with him. He watched her head swing towards him and he opened his mouth to speak, but her glance swept over him and she turned to follow the others.

A movement outside one of the classroom's tall, narrow windows made him look out. One boy was already in the yard, and the snow was thick and inviting. Beyond the railings there was the village and, through a gap in the houses, he could see the flat fens stretching away in a desert of whiteness. He knew it all. He had not lost his memory. The stuffiness of the classroom was to blame—and outside there was delicious coolness, and space. Without bothering to follow the others to the cloakroom for his coat, he went out.

There was still only the boy in the playground; a new kid kicking up snow. He was finding the soft patches, not already trodden, and, as he ploughed into them, he made the snow smoke around his ankles so that he almost seemed to lack feet.

Ben went across to him and said, "They let you out early, did they?"

The new kid raised his head and looked at the others who were now crowding out through the door. "I reckon," he said.

"Me an' all," said Ben. It wasn't strictly true, but he didn't mind bending the truth a bit as he had been feeling ill. But not anymore. "Where d'you come from?" he asked.

"Over yonder." The new kid nodded vaguely beyond

the railings and then went back to kicking snow. "It's warm, ain't it?" he said, watching the powder drift around his knees. "When you get used to it."

"What do your dad do?"

"Horseman," said the kid, and that was enough to tell Ben where he lived and where his father worked. Only one farm for miles had working horses. Tommy's family, the Drakes, had always had horses and were rich enough to have them working alongside tractors, as a kind of hobby.

"You live along Pingle Bank, then," said Ben. The horseman had a cottage there near the edge of the big drainage canal, the Pingle, that cut a straight, deep channel across the flat fens.

"That's right," said the kid, and looked up at the sky. "More of it comin'."

The clouds had thickened over the winter sun and, in the grey light, snow had begun to fall again. The kid held his face up to it. "Best time o' the year, winter. Brings you out into the open, don't it?"

"Reckon," Ben agreed. "If them clouds was in summer we should be gettin' soaked."

"I hate gettin' wet." The kid's face was pale, and snow was resting on his eyelashes.

"Me an' all."

They stood side by side and let the snow fall on them. The kid was quite right; it seemed warm.

Then the snowball fight rolled right up to them and charging through the middle of it came Tommy, pulling Ben's sister on her sledge. Just like him to have taken over the sledge and Jenny and barge into the new kid as though he was nobody. Ben stooped, rammed snow into two hard fistfuls and hurled them with all his force at Tommy's red face. He was usually a good shot but he missed, and Tommy was yelling at Jenny as she labored to make snowballs and pile them on the sledge.

"They ain't no good! Look, they're fallin' apart." Tommy crouched and swept them all back into the snow.

Jenny had no height but a lot of temper. She was on her feet, her face as red as his, and yanked her sledge away.

"Bring that back!" he yelled, but Ben was already charging at him.

Tommy must have been off balance because it took no more than a touch to push him sideways and send him into the snow flat on his back.

"You want to leave my sister alone." Ben sat on his chest with his knees on Tommy's arms. "Tell her you're sorry."

He and Tommy were the same size, both strong, and sometimes they banged their heads together just to see who would be the first to back off. But this time, without any effort or even bothering to answer him, Tommy sat up and spilled Ben off his chest as though he had no weight at all. And, as he tilted back helplessly, Ben saw the new kid standing by, watching.

"Hi!" he shouted. "Snowball fight. You're on my side."

The kid looked pretty useful; pale, but solid. And Ben needed help.

"You done it wrong," the new kid said to Ben and, without hurrying, he stepped forward.

The kid reached out to where Tommy was still sitting

and put a hand over his face, spreading out pale, cold fingers across his mouth and eyes. He seemed merely to stroke him, but Tommy fell backwards.

"You don't need no pressure," said the kid. "All you got to do is let 'em know you're there."

"You got him!" Ben had rolled away to let the kid tackle Tommy alone. "Show us your stuff!"

The kid seemed to be in no hurry, and Tommy lay where he was, one startled eye showing between the pallid fingers. Any second now and there would be a quick thrust of limbs and Tommy would send the kid flying. It was stupid to wait for it; Ben started forward to stop the massacre.

But then the kid looked up. The snow was still in his eyelashes, and a crust of it was at the corners of his mouth, like ice.

"Want me to do any more?" he asked.

In the rest of the playground, shouts of snowfights echoed against the high windows and dark walls of the old school building, but in this corner the grey clouds seemed to hang lower as if to deaden the kid's voice.

"I asked you," he said. "You want to see me do some more?"

Tommy stirred, gathering himself to push. In a moment the boy would pay for being so careless, unless he had some trick and was pressing on a nerve. Ben wanted to see what would happen. He nodded.

The kid did not look away from Ben, but his hand left Tommy's face. And Tommy did not get up. He simply lay there with his eyes and mouth wide open. He looked scared.

The kid, still crouching, began to stroke the snow. He curved his fingers and raked it, dusting the white powder into Tommy's hair, then over his brow and his eyes; and then the kid's hand, so pale it could not be seen in the snow, was over Tommy's lips, and snow was being thrust into the gaping mouth. The kid leant over him and Tommy was terrified. He tried to shout, but more snow was driven into his mouth. He rolled over, thrashing helplessly.

The kid paused as though waiting for instructions. But Ben, curious to see what Tommy would do, waited.

It was then that the brittle little sound of a handbell reached them. It came from the porch where Miss Carter was calling them in. But suddenly the sound ceased, and even the shouting of the snowfights died. The whole play-ground had seen her drop the bell.

She started forward, pushing her way through the crowds, and then, caught up in her anxiety, they came with her like black snowflakes on the wind.

It was Tommy, jerking and choking on the ground, that drew them. It was no natural fooling in the snow. He was fighting to breathe. And the new kid stood over him, looking down.

"Tommy, what have you done!" Miss Carter was stooping over him, crying out at the sight of his mouth wide open and full of whiteness. "Oh my God!"

Ben stared across her bent back at the new kid. He simply stood where he was, a sprinkle of white in the short crop of his black hair, and gazed back at him.

"Who did this to you?" Miss Carter had thrust her fingers into the snow-gape in Tommy's face, and rolled

34

him over so that he was coughing, gasping, and heaving all at once. "How did it happen?"

But he could not answer and she helped him to his feet and began walking with him.

"Who saw it? Which of you did this?" She had snow in her fur-lined boots and her grey hair was untidy. Her little red nose was sharp with the cold and she pointed it around the ring that had gathered, sniffing out the guilty one. "You?" Her eyes were on Ben but had passed by almost before he had shaken his head. "What about you?" The new kid was at the back of the crowd and did not even have to answer.

Denials came from every side, and the chattering crowd followed her into school.

Ben and the kid hung back, and were alone in the porch when the door closed and shut them out. Neither had said a word, and Ben turned towards him. The kid stood quite still gazing straight ahead as though the door was the open page of a book and he was reading it. He wore a long black jacket, and a grey scarf was wound once around his neck and hung down his back. Ben noticed for the first time that the kid's black trousers were knee-length and were tucked into long, thick socks. They looked like riding breeches, and he thought the kid must help his father with the horses. But his boots were big and clumsy, not elegant like a horseman's. There was something gawky about him; he looked poor and old-fashioned.

"You done all right," said Ben. "Tommy ain't bad in a fight."

The kid turned towards him. There was still unmelted

35

snow on his cheeks, and his eyelashes were tinged with white. His dark eyes were liquid as though he was on the verge of crying, but that was false. They had no expression at all. "He ain't as good as he reckon," said the kid, and left it at that.

"What class you in?" Ben asked.

"Same as you."

"Didn't notice you."

"I were by the stove."

"Miss Carter always keep her bum to that, that's why it don't throw out no heat," said Ben, but the kid did not smile. He led the way inside.

They had not been missed. Miss Carter was still fussing around Tommy. She had pulled the fireguard back from the stove so that he could go to the front of the class and sit close to it. But she was still angry.

"I'm going to catch whoever did that to you, and when I do . . ." She pinched in her little mouth until it was lipless and her eyes needled around the room.

Ben had taken his usual place at the back, and suddenly he realized the new kid had wandered off. He searched, and found him. He was sitting at a desk no more than two paces from Miss Carter and Tommy. He had one arm over the desk lid, and the other resting loosely on the back of his chair. He was quite untroubled.

"Stand up, Tommy," Miss Carter ordered. "Now turn round and point out who did this terrible thing."

Tommy, a hero now, was enjoying himself. He faced the class. Ben could see the pale curve of the new kid's cheek and guessed at the deep-water look of the eyes that were turned on Tommy.

36

"Tommy!" said Miss Carter, and obediently Tommy looked round the room. He smirked at several people but not at Ben. He ignored him as though angry with him for what had happened yet not prepared to betray him. But there was a real risk he would get his revenge on the kid. Yet again his glance went by as though the boy's desk was empty, and he said, "Nobody done it. I just fell over, that's all."

The girl next to Ben whispered to her friend, "Maybe he had a fit. That looked like it with his mouth all white. Like he was foaming."

"Be quiet!" Miss Carter had lost her patience. "Sit down!" she ordered Tommy, and for the rest of the afternoon she was savage, even with him.

From time to time Ben looked towards the new kid, but he kept his head bowed over his work and Ben saw no more than the black bristles of his cropped hair. Nobody attempted to speak to him because whenever anybody moved, Miss Carter snapped.

The last half-hour dragged, but then, with a rattle of pencils and a banging of desk lids, the afternoon ended. The new kid wasted no time. He was out of the door ahead of everybody else, and Ben did not catch him until he was halfway across the playground.

"Where you going?" he asked.

"The Pingle."

"We ain't supposed to. Because of the ice."

"I live there."

Then Ben remembered the horseman's cottage on the bank, but he said, "Ain't you going to hang around here a bit? We got some good slides in the yard."

37

"Ice is better."

The others, charging out at the door, prevented Ben saying more. Jenny, with her sledge, was being chased by Tommy. He was himself again and was telling her, "Your sledge will go great on the Pingle."

"I don't want to go," she said.

A bigger girl butted in. "You heard what Miss Carter said, Tommy Drake. Ain't you got no sense?"

Tommy paid no attention. "Come on, Jenny. I ain't got time to go home and fetch me skates, or else I would. I'll bring 'em tomorrow and you can have a go. Promise."

She was tempted, but she said, "I don't want to go there. And you know why."

"I won't take a step on it unless it's rock hard," said Tommy.

"I ain't going," said Jenny.

At the school gate, the kid moved his feet impatiently on the step. It had been cleared of snow and the metal studs on his boots rattled.

Tommy had also lost his patience. "If she cracks she bears, if she bends she breaks. Everybody know that's true, no matter what old Carter say. And I won't budge away from the bank unless it's safe."

"No," said Jenny.

Suddenly the kid kicked at the steps and made sparks fly from the sole of his boot, and Tommy looked up. The wind dived over the school roof in a howl and a plunge of snow, and the kid's voice merged with it as he yelled, "Come on!"

He and Ben ran together, and Tommy grabbed at the sledge and made for the gate. Several others came with him.

Ben and the boy kept ahead of the rest as they rounded the corner into the lane. Traffic had failed to churn up the snow and had packed it hard, almost icy, so it would have been as good as anywhere for Jenny's sledge; but Ben ran with the boy between hedges humped and white, and the others followed.

They left the road just before it climbed to the bridge across the Pingle, and they stood at the top of the bank, looking down. They were the first to come here. The grass blades, slowly arching as the snow had added petal after petal through the day, supported an unbroken roof just clear of the ground. Below them, the straight, wide channel stretched away to left and right through the flat, white land. The water had become a frozen road, and the wind had swept it almost clear, piling the snow in an endless, smooth drift on the far side.

Tommy had come up alongside them. "You could go for miles!" he shouted.

But Jenny hung back. "I don't like it." The air was grey and cold and it almost smothered her small voice. "I want to go home."

"It ain't dark yet." His voice yelped as though it came from the lonely seagull that angled up on a frozen gust far out over the white plain. He began to move forward. "Let's get down there."

"She doesn't want to go." Ben was close to him, but Tommy paid no heed. "Nobody's going down that bank, Tommy." Ben stepped forward, blocking his way. "Nobody!"

Tommy came straight on. His eyes met Ben's but their expression did not change. His whole attention was focused on the ice below and his gaze seemed to go through Ben as though he was not there.

In a sudden cold anger Ben lowered his head and lunged with both arms. He thrust at Tommy's chest with all his force. His fingers touched, but in the instant of touching they lost their grip. He thrust with all his power, but it was air alone that slid along his arms and fingers, and Tommy was past and through and plunging down the bank.

The kid, watching him, said, "You still don't do it right."

Tommy had taken Jenny's sledge with him, and at the ice edge he turned and shouted to them up the bank. "Come on, all of you!"

"No!" Ben stood in front of them. "Don't go!" He opened his arms, but they came in a group straight for him. "Stop!" They did not answer. Their eyes did not look directly at him. They pushed into him, like a crush of cattle, pretending he was not there. He clutched at one after another but the strange weakness he had felt earlier made him too flimsy to stop anything and they were beyond him and going down to join Tommy.

"I got to teach you a few things," said the kid.

"I don't feel too good," said Ben. "I think I ought to go home."

The boy gazed at him for a moment with eyes that again seemed to be rimmed with frost, and shook his head. "There's them down there to see to," he said.

Slowly, Ben nodded. He had to think of Jenny.

They went down together and found Tommy still on the bank. Frozen reeds stood up through the ice and there was a seepage of water at the edge that made them all hesitate. All except the new kid. He put one foot on it, testing.

"If she cracks she bears," he said.

Ben watched. The boy had plenty of courage. He was leaning forward now, putting all his weight on the ice.

"She cracks," he said.

But Ben had heard nothing. "No," he called out. "She bends."

He was too late. The boy had stepped out onto the ice. Then Ben heard the crack under his boots, and the echo of it ringing from bank to bank and away along the endless ice in thin winter music.

The boy moved out until he was a figure in black in the middle of the channel. "She bears," he called out, and Ben, who knew he could never stop the others now, stepped out to be with him.

There was no crack this time, but the ice held. He could feel the gentle pulse of it as he walked towards the middle. There was something almost like a smile on the new kid's face. "Both on us done it," he said, and Ben nodded.

On the bank there was a squabble. The big girl, protecting Jenny, was trying to pull the sledge rope from Tommy. "Let her have her sledge," she said. "You didn't ought to have brung her here."

"It's safe enough."

"I don't care whether it's safe or not, you didn't ought to have brung her. Not Jenny, of all people."

"Why all the fuss about Jenny?" said Ben to the kid. "I don't know what they're going on about."

"Don't you?" The kid's eyes, darkening as the day

dwindled, rested on him. Far away along the length of the frozen channel, snow and sky and darkness joined.

"Why don't they come out here?" said Ben. "They can see us."

"We can go and fetch 'em," said the kid.

"How?"

"Get hold of that sledge. They'll follow."

Ben hesitated. Perhaps he was too weak to do even that.

The kid saw his doubt, and said, "You've pulled a sledge before, ain't you?" Ben nodded. "Well, all you got to do is remember what it feel like. That's all."

Ben had to rely on him. Everything he had tried himself had gone wrong. He walked across to where Tommy was still arguing.

"See what you done to her," the girl was saying. She had her arm around Jenny's shoulder and Jenny was crying, snuffling into her gloves. "Ain't you got no feelings, Tommy Drake?"

"Well, just because it happened once," said Tommy, "that ain't to say it's going to happen again."

"Wasn't just once!" The girl thrust her head forward, accusing him. "There was another time." She lifted her arm from Jenny's shoulder and pointed up the bank behind her. "There was a boy lived up there, along Pingle Bank; he came down here and went through the ice one winter time, and they never found him till it thawed."

"That were a long time ago," said Tommy. "Years before any of us was born."

"You ought to know about that if anybody do, Tommy Drake. That boy's father worked on your farm. Every-

42

body know about that even if it was all them years ago. His father were a horseman and lived along the bank."

"Hey!" Ben was close to Tommy. "Just like the new kid."

But even that did not make Tommy turn his way. Ben reached for the sledge rope and jerked it. He felt the rope in his fingers just before it slipped through and fell, but he had tugged it from Tommy's grasp and the sledge ran out on to the ice.

"Come on, Tommy," he said. "Come with me and the new kid."

The girl was watching the sledge and accusing Tommy. "What did you want to do that for?"

"I didn't," he said.

"I did it," said Ben, but nobody looked towards him.

The girl was furious with Tommy. "Just look what you done. Now you'll have to leave it."

Tommy had put one foot on the ice, testing it. "I ain't frit,"he said. "I reckon it'll hold."

"Of course it will," Ben encouraged him. "We're both out here, ain't we?" He paused and looked over his shoulder to make sure, but the kid was still there, watching. "Two of us. Me and him."

Tommy had both feet on the ice and had taken another step. "See," he called to the others on the bank. "Nothing to it."

"Don't you make a parade out there by yourself any longer, Tommy Drake." The girl pulled Jenny's face tighter into her shoulder and made an effort to muffle Jenny's ears. She leant forward as far as she could, keeping her voice low so that Jenny should not hear. "Can't you see

43

what you're doing to her? This were just the place where Ben went through the ice last winter."

Tommy, stamping to make the ice ring beneath him, kept his back to her. "If she cracks," he said, "she bears. If she bends, she breaks."

"Can't you hear?" said the girl. "This is just the place where Ben were drowned!"

The snow came in a sudden flurry, putting a streaked curtain between Ben and the rest of them. It was then that he remembered. He remembered everything. The kid had come up to stand beside him, and they stood together and watched.

The ice under Tommy sagged as they knew it would. They heard the soft rending as it split, and they saw its broken edge rear up. They heard the yell and the slither, and remembered the cold gulp of the black water that, with years between, had swallowed each of them. But now it was somebody else who slid under.

Then Jenny's scream reached Ben through the wind that was pushing down the channel as the night came on. She should be at home; not out here watching this. He stooped to the sledge and pushed.

On the bank they saw nothing but a tight spiral of snow whipped up from the ice, but the sledge slid into the water beside Tommy and floated. He grabbed at it.

From out on the ice they saw the girl, held by the others, reach from the bank and grasp the rope, and then Tommy, soaking and freezing, crawled into the white snow and made it black. They watched as the whole group, sobbing and murmuring, climbed the bank, showed for a few moments against the darkening sky, and were gone.

In the empty channel the two figures stood motionless. Their eyes gazed unblinking through the swirl as the snow came again, hissing as it blew between the frozen reeds.

Aidan Chambers

Seeing Is Believing

No one was more surprised than I when Great Aunt Florence died, leaving me all her money and property. We had met only twice; when I was a little girl of eight, and again when I was fourteen. Why should she choose me out of all her many relatives to be her heiress? I've never discovered the answer. Florence was thought by all the family to be eccentric as well as formidable, and never explained her actions to anyone. So the whys and wherefores of her last will and testament must remain a mystery.

A tall, stately woman, dressed always in full-length black dresses, her hair silver white, her eyes so sharp and active you felt that every move you made was noticed, I found her frightening. For the last thirty years of her life she lived as a recluse in her enormous Georgian house, a beautiful building on the outside, but inside, dark and brooding and full of shadows. The family said she hated growing old and had hidden herself away among the heavy drapes that hung at the windows, the bulky old-fashioned furniture that crowded the high-ceilinged rooms. She died in her sleep, aged eighty-three. I was twenty at the time, and it seemed to me that a last remnant of old Victorian England died with her.

Aunt Florence's solicitor told me I had inherited the house, Compton Court, and all the money—about ten thousand pounds—left over from her estate when the government had taken its share in death duties.

When the shock wore off, I settled down to decide what to do with my unexpected wealth. Everyone was, of course, full of good advice. My parents, the solicitor, my relatives, my friends. After weeks of hearing what other people would do with my money if they had it, I began to wish Aunt Florence had left the lot to charity.

One thing was certain. The house would have to be sold. I could not live there; the place wasn't my style at all, and anyway I had my own life to lead and did not want to be tied to an old house and all the problems it would bring with it.

Getting rid of Compton Court was no easy matter, however. And the difficulties began with pompous Mr. Pearce, Aunt Florence's ponderous solicitor.

When I instructed him to sell the house, he coughed and shuffled his pin-striped bottom in his chair, and looked as though he had been told to sell rotten eggs.

"What's the matter?" I said. "Don't say you are like everyone else and think I should live in that mausoleum of a place!"

"Not at all," he muttered in his courtroom voice. "There are . . . that is . . . a difficulty in selling the property."

I sighed. "Don't tell me! The place is eaten up with woodworm, has dry rot in every floorboard, and is likely to fall down at any minute."

The lawyer smiled faintly. (I doubt if he ever allowed himself to smile other than faintly.)

"Not a bit of it. Structurally the building is as sound as a bell. Your aunt was meticulous in her affairs and kept the house in excellent condition."

"Then what?"

More shuffling. More polite coughing. More nervous glances over his half-moon glasses.

"I'm afraid, Miss Lockwood, the house has a dreadful reputation for being haunted."

I stared at the man in disbelief; then laughed aloud.

"Oh come on, Mr. Pearce! Surely people don't get hooked on ghosts anymore!"

Pearce was not amused.

"You may laugh. Surprisingly, however, people do get . . . hooked . . . on ghosts. *Sometimes* haunted houses fetch very good prices just because they are haunted . . ."

"But?"

"To be frank, Miss Lockwood . . ."

"I wish you would be, Mr. Pearce."

"Your aunt's house . . . that is, *your* house . . . has a reputation for being haunted by a far from pleasant ghost and . . ."

He paused. I could see just where his lawyer's convoluted mind was leading me.

"People like nice ghosts but not nasty ones. So houses with nasty ghosts inside them don't sell for high prices. Right?"

Pearce nodded. "If at all," he said, drawing in breath

to emphasize the unspoken thought that *I* was one of the people who could expect *never* to sell my ghost-inhabited property.

"Now look, Mr. Pearce," I said firmly. "I think all this ghost business is nonsense . . ."

"That is all very well, Miss Lockwood," Pearce interrupted, and went on just as firmly, "but too many other people do not agree. You wish to *sell* Compton Court, not *buy* it."

One up to Pearce. I sat in my chair and glared at him across his ancient mahogany desk, disliking all lawyers, and Pearce in particular at that moment, for their infernal knack of winning arguments.

"What should I do, then?" I asked after an awkward silence.

"There are a number of possibilities," he said, leaning forward and in his element now. He had got his way—or so he thought—and could now plan my decisions for me. "You could take a chance, put the property on the open market, and wait until you got a reasonable price. I would advise against this. You could turn the house into flats and let them, hoping alterations would change the . . . er . . . unsavory atmosphere of the place. A reasonable course of action this, but costly and time-consuming. It would be years before you recovered your capital outlay. I advise you to reject this plan. Finally, you could pull the house down and sell the site for redevelopment. The advantages are many: a quickly acquired sum of money probably running into five figures; little administrative bother; and the problem solved for good and all. I advise this as your wisest solution."

The idea of another old house being turned into a warren of flats or, worse still, being replaced by a glass-and-concrete office block suddenly put fight back into me.

"Stop right there," I said. "You say this place is haunted?"

"I say nothing, Miss Lockwood," Pearce said, running true to lawyer's form. "I only say it has a *reputation* . . ."

"O.K. Put it how you like," I snapped. "Well, I say it isn't. It's all baloney. And I'll prove it. I'll live there a couple of months—more if necessary—and settle the matter once and for all. Maybe opening the place up a bit will work wonders. And perhaps then we can find a buyer who isn't put off by rumors."

Pearce shrugged his shoulders.

"It's your house, Miss Lockwood. I can only offer my advice."

I smiled and stood up.

"That's right, Mr. Pearce. It is! And you can!"

So I went to live at Compton Court after all, arriving in late summer to begin my two-month, self-imposed ghost hunt. The house had been kept habitable by a housekeeper and her husband, an old couple who had tended Aunt Florence for years and lived in a small house adjoining the Court. Mrs. Truelove did the cleaning and cooking; her husband, Albert, saw to the gardens and did the odd jobs. Since Aunt's death they had continued life as though she were still there, carrying on the household routines because no one had told them to stop.

They welcomed me warmly, chatted about Florence, whom they seemed genuinely fond of, and then, by hints and oblique questions, made it clear that they feared I might dismiss them. I reassured the old couple; they were a homely pair, and I knew from Pearce that they lived entirely on the wages Florence paid them. They would, I realized, pose a problem when the house was sold; but I decided to cross that bridge when I came to it.

As soon as I had settled in, I toured the house, accompanied by Mrs. Truelove. We began in the basement with its palatial kitchen kept as clean as a new pin, the pantries and storerooms. "And down there?" I asked as we passed a door in the back passage.

"Only the way into the cellars, Miss," said Mrs. Truelove. " 'Tain't used for nothing. A cobwebby place."

She hustled me on.

"I'd like to inspect it all the same," I said.

Mrs. Truelove sniffed—a habit of hers, I soon learned, when she disagreed with something.

"Nothing to see. Come upstairs and I'll show you the living-rooms."

There were five ground-floor rooms, large, beautifully proportioned, but shrouded in curtained gloom: a drawing-room, dining-room, library and a couple of reception rooms. Redecorated and refurnished in the right style, they would have been showplaces.

Upstairs there were eight bedrooms of various sizes, a couple with their own dressing-rooms and bathrooms. And above these, attics used once as servants' quarters and now full of the accumulated junk which Florence would never allow anyone to get rid of. On Portobello Road the stuff would bring a small fortune, and I made a note to find a buyer once I'd removed a few oddments which took my fancy.

The tour of inspection over, I went with Mrs. Truelove

for a cup of tea in the kitchen. As we sat together at the scrubbed deal table, Mrs. Truelove chattering away about one thing after another, I thought about the house I'd inherited. It was easy to see why people said it was haunted: the deep shadows that lurked everywhere could—if you wanted them to—seem menacing; the floors creaked, often without anyone walking on them; and a heavy silence, caused no doubt by the thick curtains that hung everywhere, wrapped the house in an eerie stillness despite its being almost in the center of town.

After a couple of days, when I'd grown used to the place, and was on easy terms with Mrs. Truelove, I broached the subject of ghosts while the pair of us were preparing lunch.

"Oh yes," she said, " 'tis haunted sure enough. Miss Florence said 'twas."

"And what about you?" I asked, a little irritated at the hearsay which always seemed to creep into any conversation about the supernatural. "Have you seen a ghost yourself?"

Mrs. Truelove peered at me over the lettuce she was chopping.

"Don't believe me then?"

"It isn't that, Mrs. T. I just like evidence for things such as ghosts. Seeing is believing, and all that."

"Stay here long enough and you'll see!"

"See what?"

She sniffed. " 'Tain't good to talk about it."

"Give me a clue, then." I couldn't keep the mockery out of my voice.

"All I say," Mrs. Truelove replied in the tone of someone putting an end to an unpleasant subject before anyone takes offense, "all I say is that you should keep out of yon cellar on Friday nights."

I stared at her, unsure whether to treat what she had said seriously or to laugh.

"Mrs. T.! You don't mean to tell me . . ."

"I don't mean to tell you nothin'. And if you'll pass me the 'taters, Miss, I'll get to peelin' them."

"Now wait a minute . . ."

"I thought you'd maybe like a nice bit of fresh salmon for lunch."

"Look . . . I only want to . . ."

Mrs. Truelove clattered the salad bowl down on the dresser.

"Now see here, Miss. I don't mean to give no offense. But if you don't mind, I'll say no more than I have already about hauntin'. 'Tis dangerous talk and you'll sleep sounder in the night for putting such matters out of your head."

I gave up. There was little point in annoying the old dear, who was plainly upset by the thought of ghosts. Anyway, I had something to go on: Friday nights in the cellar! The whole business was beginning to sound like a Victorian gothic melodrama.

Well, I thought, I've got to survive this place for a couple of months; I might as well enjoy myself.

Truth to tell, the excitement was catching hold of me. Everyone was so damnably certain the house was haunted that my resolve to prove them wrong was more firm than ever. And if the ghost wouldn't come to me, why I'd go to the ghost! I waited impatiently for Friday night.

You'll have gathered by now that I'm not the nervous

53

type, that I think (correction: *thought*) ghosts little more than the fanciful creations of old women's dreams—a giggle, no less; and that my own imagination is, to say the least, somewhat dull. (I never did very well in English at school. I could spell and all that; but when it came to writing stories I was a dud!) Nevertheless, I must emphasize this point. You'll see why later.

I must also tell you about my dog, because he comes into this account in a minute. Buccaneer—Buccy for short—is one of those over-large, over-affectionate boxer dogs who sit on settees, looking like Winston Churchill without his cigar. But I adore him, and take him wherever I go—a chronic case of "love me—love my dog," which has rather too often meant that boyfriends have preferred not to. Buccy is possessive. It isn't that he growls or bites or is in any way vicious. Just the opposite. Which is what causes the trouble. As soon as there is a hint of cozy companionship in the air, Buccy wants his share, and snuggles up. Boyfriends find him disconcerting. He has a knack of pushing between them and me just at the tender moments, and no one ever manages to shift him. (I can never bring myself to order him out of the room—his great, slobbering face melts my sternness and he wins!) So, of course, Buccy went with me to Compton Court. Mrs. Truelove took to him and spoilt him by feeding him choice bones. Albert spent more time romping with him in the garden than tending to the odd jobs; and when Buccy wasn't either eating Mrs. Truelove's bones, or thundering round the flowerbeds after Albert, he padded along at my feet like an attendant footman—a footman of a very snooty, nose-in-the-air kind too. It was having him with me, I think, which prevented my feeling at all afraid of sleeping alone in that huge master bedroom during the first night or two of my stay. He is such a constant, comforting companion that I never stop to think what life would be like without him. Which is partly why that Friday night's events were so terrifying. For Buccy deserted me early in the proceedings, the coward—though his flight from the scene was indeed a proof that discretion is the better part of valor, and I wish I had taken his hint.

Friday came. Mrs. Truelove left at about eight-thirty. I went round the house securing doors and windows, and checking every room. I wanted to be quite sure there was nothing that could accidentally be interpreted as a "ghost." I've heard too many stories about hauntings which investigation showed were no more than the work of stray cats or trapped birds or bits of furniture blown down by the breeze from an open window, to be taken in by such things. All was safe, locked, firmly set in its proper place.

But as I went round, one thing did strike me. The house seemed even more gloomy than ever, the shadows deeper, as though the darkness in corners here and there was not caused by the absence of light, but was itself a solid thing. At the time, I put this down to the greyness of the evening outside and my heightened expectation that something on this day was going to happen—for I must admit that, despite my usually calm temperament, I was already a little nervy, just the least bit on tenterhooks. I was aware that my heart was beating faster than usual and my stomach gave the occasional flutter when I thought of the cellar.

Nothing daunted, I pressed on. Downstairs I went, to the basement kitchen where only a few moments before

I had been bantering with Mrs. Truelove while we washed up the dinner things. Now, about nine-thirty, the room seemed quite changed. Nothing had moved—all was as I had left it—but there was an indefinable . . . *something*: an atmospheric tingle as though electricity was sparking about unseen. The shadows here were even more thick, more tangible than those upstairs. I could not even see the corners of the room.

As I entered, Buccy's hackles rose and he whimpered. I cannot remember seeing this happen more than half a dozen times in as many years, and always only when other, usually snappy, dogs were teasing him. But now he whined and slunk up to me, his eyes wild, his ears down, and pressed himself against my legs.

I patted him.

"Silly chap," I muttered. "Frightened of shadows?"

As much for my own benefit as for Buccy's, however, I picked up Mrs. Truelove's rolling pin from the pastry bench, went to each corner in turn, and tapped the walls.

I laughed, and said aloud to Buccy, who was still slinking along at my feet:

"There, look! What's to be afraid of?"

Reassured myself, even if Buccy wasn't, I left the kitchen and walked along the back passage to the cellar door. As I opened it, Buccy started shaking violently, and began to whine in terror. I tried to calm him, and though he stopped making such a noise, the trembling went on unabated.

I opened the cellar door, and groped in the dark for the light switch, found it and flicked it on. I shall never understand about cellars—why they must always be so ill lit. This one was no exception. A dim glow from a bulb in the cellar below found its way round the twist in the cellar steps. It was all I had to see by in climbing down the worn, stone slabs of the stairs, slabs so worn they seemed far older than the rest of the house.

"Come on, Buccy," I said as loudly and as cheerfully as I could. "Let's go."

I began the descent into the cellar, groping with one hand against the dusty wall, and the other, I realized suddenly, still gripping the rolling pin and holding it at the ready.

Five or six steps down, and Buccy's whimpering cries told me he was not following.

I stopped and turned. There he stood, at the cellar door, fear and his desire to be with me battling in him.

"Now, Buccy," I said in a lecturing manner. "I'm going down here, I don't care what you think. So you jolly well make your mind up that you are coming too."

Buccy sat down, his eyes crazed with fright. I'd never seen him like this before.

Climbing back to him, I sat on the passage floor and rubbed his jowly face.

"Dear Buccy," I mumbled into his ear, "I've *got* to go down, old chap. I know it's a bit grisly and dark. But I can't let that put me off. There's nothing to be afraid of, honest. Except maybe a mouse or two, and you don't mind that, even if I do. Won't you come?"

I got up, gave him a final, encouraging pat, and went a couple of steps down.

Buccy did not move. His tongue hung out, he panted and shook and altogether looked a pitiful sight.

57

"Oh, all right, stay there!" I said, my own nervousness putting a biting edge to my words which I did not intend. Then by an effort of will, I turned from him and made my way into the cellar.

There were shadows aplenty there! It was a large room, with walls of rough-hewn stone that long ago had been whitewashed but were now coated with black dust and draped with cobwebs that hung everywhere like broken, dirty lace. The ceiling was low—even I, at five feet three, had almost to stoop to avoid the heavy beams that supported it. The floor was made of stone slabs, uneven and worn.

What surprised me more than anything was that the room was empty. I had expected the kind of rubbish people put in cellars: coal, or old boxes, broken furniture, and discarded tools. But, no; there was nothing, not even a stick of firewood.

How I wished Buccy was with me! I called him, softly, and whistled, and clicked my tongue. But nothing would bring him down; his whining went on plaintively, drifting to me from the back passage.

"Traitor!" I muttered to myself.

Then something small and black and very quick darted across the floor. Strangling the scream that rose in my throat, I dashed towards it and struck the floor with the rolling pin. The noise echoed hollowly in the cavernlike room. At once numerous other black objects scudded away in all directions.

Beetles!

I shivered at the sight of them and stood staring, astonished at the way they vanished into chinks and cracks I could hardly see.

But at least beetles are living creatures, I thought, trying to milk a little comfort from the incident.

I looked round me again. There was nothing to be seen in this room to arouse any suspicions. Unpleasant and creepy it might be, but not haunted.

In the far wall, there was an arch which led through to a smaller room, no more than a big cavity. I advanced inside with little liking, but determined to leave no ghost unturned.

The place was about a dozen feet long and half that wide. The ceiling was even lower than in the main cellar, and dipped down from the sides to the middle, where it was about an inch higher than my head. It looked as though a great weight was pressing on it from above, bending it down in the middle. I had the uncomfortable sensation as I stood beneath that ceiling that at any moment it might cave in.

The light from the bulb in the main cellar shone through the arched entrance, giving me just enough illumination to see by. Clearly this had once been the wine vault, where the casks had been stored. At least, that was what I decided, seeing no other reason for such a strange little, almost dungeonlike room.

As I glanced about, my eyes caught sight of the stone slabs in the center of the floor. They were cleaner, newer than the rest, as though they had been laid much more recently. Four or five of them were like this, covering a strip of ground six feet or so long and three or so wide.

59

I next became aware that the air here was intensely damp, so damp it was clogging in my throat and lungs. This too seemed odd, for when I touched the walls they were quite dry, without a trace of slime or moisture.

Perhaps, I thought, there is a vent through which the damp air is flowing.

I went round, tapping both walls and drooping roof with the rolling pin, looking for openings, and listening for the hollow sound that would betray a cavity behind the fabric. Nothing; all solid, firm stone.

Then I realized that, without thinking, I had pulled my handkerchief from my sleeve and was holding it to my mouth and nose, as if to protect myself from a bad smell. I took the handkerchief away and sniffed the air. Immediately, a nauseating sweet-sour odor set me coughing and retching.

I put the handkerchief to my nose and mouth again at once, and retreated out of the inner cellar into the main one.

For the first time in my life I was now truly, deeply afraid. I could not begin to explain my fear. But suddenly I knew what Buccy felt and wished above anything to get out of this place. Cold chills and waves of shivers ran through me.

"Buccy!" I called, my voice shrill with desperation, and made a dash for the stairs.

But I took no more than two or three stumbling strides before the sound of a loud crash stopped me in my tracks. I could not tell where the noise had come from, and this made it all the more uncanny. But I knew it was not of Buccy's making, and, far more frightening, knew beyond doubt, that the crashing noise and the disgusting, sickening smell and the damp air of the small cellar behind me were all in some inexplicable way linked together.

By now I no longer had complete control of myself. I was shaking violently, my teeth were chattering, my legs went limp. I opened my mouth to call again to Buccy but the sound would not come.

Rooted to the spot, trembling on the verge of hysteria, I waited, panting, expecting every second to hear the crash again.

What next took my attention was something indescribably worse. I saw, on the cellar steps, where they twisted round into my view, a shape emerge, as though created from the thick air of the cellar before my disbelieving eyes. At first I could pick out no detail; all I saw was a lurid glow, nothing more. But I knew that, whatever it was, the thing was evil, malicious, foul.

As I watched—I could do nothing else for I was unable to move a muscle; the power to do so had left me—the indeterminate shape began to come towards me. Its progress was slow, slithering almost, secretive. Disgusting.

On it came inch by inch, foot by foot. Its approach seemed everlasting, and I felt my life from now on and for ever was to be spent in watching its unceasing progress towards me.

And as it came I began to distinguish features, details; began to see what it was.

How do you describe a half-decayed corpse? For this was what I saw. A woman's corpse, her rotting grave clothes swathing her body, covering almost all her form. From her head fell tumbling about her face and shoulders long, matted hair. Through her hair I could see, as the specter came within three feet of me, the hideous face. The skin was shriveled on the bone; the eyes were empty black sockets; and the teeth grinned through a lipless mouth.

At the very moment I thought this awful . . . thing . . . would touch me, it turned, slid by, and made for the smaller room beyond, into which it went, and stood over the patch of stones I had noticed were newer than the rest.

I watched as though compelled to do so. And now, looking back on that night, I can hardly believe what next occurred. With a rending noise that echoed about my ears like the worst thunder imaginable, the ceiling of the smaller room caved in, and fell upon the ghostly figure, burying it in a cascade of stone and rubble.

What happened after this I do not know. I have no memory of leaving the cellar, of climbing the stairs or indeed of doing anything else. I suppose I must either have fled in blind terror, or fainted, and, coming to later, stumbled out of the place before regaining full consciousness. Whatever I did, all I know is that at one o'clock that night I found myself slumped on the kitchen floor with Buccy sitting at my head, looking hardly less afraid than when I had last seen him.

Shaken to the depths of my being, I managed to drag myself to my feet and make myself a cup of strong, sweet tea, before hauling myself to bed, where I slept fitfully with Buccy lying, shivering still, across the bottom of the bed.

Next morning I felt washed out and sore, and my head ached. I would have loved to lie in bed all day and recuperate. But I knew I must behave as though everything was quite normal. In fact, I was very anxious about the fallen ceiling in the cellar. Even so, nothing would have persuaded me to go down and inspect the damage.

Mrs. Truelove was busy with breakfast when I got down-stairs; Albert was cleaning out the ashes from the Aga cooker. I said good morning and sat at the table. For a moment I wanted desperately to tell them all about the night before, but managed to hold my tongue. I could just imagine Mrs. Truelove's comments! No: the best thing would be to buttonhole Albert on his own and have a talk with him. Something would have to be done about shoring up the fallen ceiling and, after all, he was employed to see to such matters. Somehow I had to discuss it with him without telling him how it had happened.

After breakfast I went for "a stroll in the garden."

Out there in the fresh morning air, the late summer sky a sparkling blue, I began to think my experience had been nothing more than a bad nightmare. Maybe I'd walked in my sleep, and that's why I found myself in the kitchen? Perhaps!

Doubts confused my mind. I sat on the lawn, lay back, and gazed at the sky. Buccy stretched himself at my side. I fondled his ears, and wondered.

And abruptly sat up.

How could I have dreamed such things? Why, I could still feel in my nose and mouth that disgusting, sickly-sweet smell.

My limbs went weak at the memory. And when I thought of that evil phantom sliding towards me, sweat broke out on my brow.

I pushed the thoughts away, stood up, and strode about the garden, frantically trying to keep myself calm, casual, unconcerned.

Buccy trotted faithfully at my heels. I crouched down and patted him.

"We've just got to know, old lad," I murmured.

He slobbered and looked contented—he'll take as much petting as anyone cares to give him, the sentimental beast!

"Mornin', Miss."

Albert's voice startled me. I jumped in surprise, tripped over my own feet, and fell backwards onto my bottom.

"Albert!" I said, laughing. "You scared the life out of me!"

"Not like you to be nervy, Miss," Albert said, and I wondered if there was more in his words than there seemed. Had he found out about the cellar and put two and two together?

I glanced suspiciously at him, but his gentle smile was just too honest to doubt. I liked old Albert; he was soft-mannered and amusing.

He bent down and patted Buccy's head. We got to chatting, discussed the weather (as always!), the news, the garden. And the garden gave me the chance I wanted. I said, casually:

"Albert, I've been meaning to ask you. I want to keep a check on the house—see it stays in good repair. But I'm hopeless at knowing about such things—damp, and woodworm, and all that stuff. Would you mind going over the place and letting me know what needs doing?"

"Course, Miss. You just say where you'd like me to start and I'll see to it all."

"I thought you might do a bit at a time, you know. There's no need to look everywhere at once."

I paused. Albert nodded agreeably.

So far, so good, I thought.

"What about starting with the cellars? You could have a look at them this morning."

"Sounds all right to me," Albert said.

"Good," I said. "That's settled, then."

I paused again. Albert went on rubbing Buccy's ears, all the while looking at me with a grin on his face that was something more than a pleasantry.

"Well," I said, standing up. "I'd better get on."

"Ah," said Albert, making no move himself.

I was about to walk away when he said quietly:

"Course, Miss, if you just wants me to see if the small cellar roof is all right, I can tell you now."

I stopped in my tracks and glanced away.

"The . . . small cellar roof?" I said, stalling for time.

"That's it," he said.

The game was up. There was no point in feigning innocence.

"You've been down there already this morning?"

He shook his head.

"Then how? . . ."

" 'Twere Friday yesterday," he said as though this explained everything.

"So?"

"I said to Mrs. T. yesterday mornin' that you'd be looking in the cellar after we went."

"What made you think that, Albert?"

"Stands to reason, don't it? . . . Mrs. T. told us about

65

your talk with her . . . about hauntin's. I knew you'd be curious."

I sat on the lawn again.

"And you let me go down there!"

"Seein's believin', you said, Miss. 'Taint no use tellin' people who say that, now is it?"

I laughed, conceding his point.

"*Touché*, Albert! But I didn't quite expect what I got."

He shrugged.

"So what do we do about the ceiling?" I asked.

"Can't do nothin', Miss."

"But we can't leave it fallen in . . ."

And then I realized. Albert had said nothing about the ceiling *falling in*. I stared at him—still the same enigmatic grin on his face.

"Look, Miss," he said at last. "The ceilin' is all right. You think it's down. But it's not. Solid as ever 'twas, you mark my words."

I was agitated again.

"But, Albert, I saw it come down. It fell on top of that . . . that . . ."

"Always does," he replied as matter of fact as if he were talking about the weather.

"You mean? . . ."

"I mean, Miss, that everybody as sees yon ghost always sees the ceilin' come down on top of it."

Suddenly I felt the relief of talking to someone about all this. At once I began to weep, and blurted out through my tears every detail of my adventure. Misadventure, rather. Dear Albert sat patiently listening, not a bit embarrassed by my weeping.

66

"I was so frightened, Albert," I said finally. "I've never been so scared. And the smell was so vile and the ghost so disgusting!"

"Don't you take on so, Miss," Albert muttered in his gentle, old man's way. " 'Tain't so terrible as you think. You knows now what's in the cellar on Friday nights, and can keep out. And, anyway, yon poor ghost won't harm you."

I blew my nose loudly into my handkerchief.

"Thanks for listening, though. You've been a help."

"That's as may be," he said. Then he chuckled. "Now you've seen . . ."

He did not have to finish the sentence. I laughed too, and nodded.

But, though I did not know it then, I had not seen everything. There was more to come.

The following Friday Albert offered to sleep in Compton Court, to give me "moral support after last week," as he put it. I should have guessed the wily old chap meant more than he said. But I let it go by.

"There's really no need," I said cheerfully. "I'll go nowhere near the cellar, I can tell you. And Buccy is good enough company. I'll be all right."

The truth is, my pride would not let me accept the old man's offer. I was determined to prove I was courageous enough to be in the same house alone with a ghost. Which just shows how much pride and ignorance go together!

The evening went by quietly. I did think the shadows were deeper than usual again, despite the glorious, bright sunset. But I told myself I was imagining it.

At eleven-thirty I went up to bed, rather pleased with

myself. Not a twinge of fear had I felt. I had heard no violent crashes from the cellars, seen not a hint of phantom figures. For an hour I read with Buccy breathing heavily in a deep sleep at my side. Then I switched off the light and was soon dead to the world.

Buccy woke me some time later when he sprang from the bed, letting out a deranged howl.

I turned on to my back and opened my eyes. And there it was! Inches from my face. An unnatural glow in the pitch-black darkness of the room. My body locked in sudden fright, and I could do nothing else but stare unblinking.

I saw a face, bloated, much larger than any face I'd ever seen before. It hung in the air above me, and there was no sign of a body, just the swollen truncated head. The eyes were sunk deep into their sockets. Thick, stringy hair fell in tangled knots from the crown of the skull. The skin on the face was blotched with festering patches, as though it had been violently bruised. The lips were drawn wide and taut across the mouth, revealing the teeth and gums so that the head seemed to grin in malice.

As I watched, the mouth opened. Inside wagged a blackened, distended tongue. And from the mouth came that same nauseating smell I had retched at in the cellar.

I wanted to scream but could not; I wanted to vomit but could not. All I could do was to lie stiff with fear and gaze at this gruesome object, helpless.

For some minutes the face remained suspended in the air only inches from me. But then, slowly, it began to shake; and as it shook, the hair and open jaw and puffed-out tongue swung and chattered and wagged about in a macabre fashion, while wave on wave of the loathsome smell belched from the mouth and wafted over my face.

How long this went on I have no idea. It seemed, at the time, to last an endless age. But then at last the specter began to move away from me, and as it went it faded in brightness and grew smaller in size, until it disappeared from sight, absorbed into the blackness of my room.

As soon as the phantom had vanished I recovered. At once the nausea left me; and I could move again.

I jumped out of bed and switched on the lights.

Buccy ran to me—he had hidden himself under a chair in the corner—and pushed himself against me, shivering still.

Together we spent the rest of the night sitting bolt upright and wide awake on my bed.

The next morning I collared Albert.

"You old tike!" I scolded him. "You knew something would happen."

"As it happens," he said, "I weren't so sure about that."

"But why didn't you tell me?"

He looked at me in his old-fashioned way.

"Now really, Miss!"

"All right—so I wouldn't have listened."

"Only some folks sees the head. Your aunt, Miss Florence, now she never did. Said 'twere all nonsense. But I sees it. So does Mrs. T."

"And so do I!" I said ruefully. "I wish I knew the explanation."

I might have known: Albert had one!

"Afore this place were built about two hundred years back," he told me, "there were a cottage on this land.

69

'Tis said an old spinster woman lived here. An old dame she were. Plenty of money. But miserly, you understand. She took in an old widow woman who had fallen on hard times. The old dame wanted company, and this were a cheap way to get it. But the old widow up and poisoned the miserly dame and buried her under the floor stones— that's the cellar now. She weren't never found out, and she got the spinster's money and the property as well.

"Well now, years later, so they say, the house got in such a poor state of repair—for the widow were as much a skinflint as the old dame she had murdered—that one night the place blew down in a great storm. And the roof fell on the widow and crushed her to death."

"So the ghost in the cellar is the specter of the old widow, standing on the grave of her victim and then being killed by the falling house; and the head upstairs is the poisoned spinster's?"

"That's how I see it, Miss."

"What an extraordinary story!"

"Aye! There ain't nowt so queer as folk!"

Well, that is what happened when I went to Compton Court to prove there are no such things as ghosts. I've never decided whether to believe Albert's explanation or not. But of this I am certain. There *are* ghosts. I've seen them.

What did I do about the house? After some trouble I found a buyer who did not believe in ghosts. Seeing, he said, is believing, and he had never seen any. I smiled, and sold the house gladly. But the strange thing is that so far he has seen nothing to convince him that my story is true. He lives happily in the house with his wife and five children, who tear round the place with endless energy.

As for Albert and Mrs. Truelove. They are still there, looking after their new employers. Mrs. Truelove spends her time telling the kids off; Albert spends most of his inventing new pranks for them to get up to.

When I last saw them both, we talked, as always, about the ghosts.

"Seein' is believin'," Albert said. "But seem's there's some who can see and some as can't."

"And a very good thing too," said Mrs. Truelove with a sniff.

Jan Mark

Absalom, Absalom

Long hair can be dangerous.

When we were children we used to thrill horribly to my mother's account of a relative who, working in a factory during the war, got her film-star coiffure tangled in the machinery and was half scalped before the charge-hand could switch off; and I was always fascinated by the Old Testament tale of Absalom, who was trapped by his hair in the branches of an oak tree, and hung there helplessly until Joab and his armor-bearers ran him through. I never quite believed that story. Surely, I thought, Absalom could have freed his head somehow; there was nothing wrong with his hands. Might he not have pulled himself up to the level of the branch, or cut himself loose? He had been in battle, after all; he would have had a sword, or at least a knife.

"Perhaps he didn't have time," said my sister Deborah, who always took the view that there was a perfectly reasonable explanation for everything. If there wasn't, she simply regarded the outrageous explanations as reasonable. "Perhaps the enemy got there just as it happened." Deborah said.

"He was the enemy, wasn't he?" I said. "Anyway, it definitely says that he *hung* there."

"Maybe there was someone hiding in the tree," said Deborah. Maybe there was.

Deborah and I spent most of our time together, although I was three years the elder. We were not popular at school. Because we lived in a big house our friends thought we must be rich, until they came to tea, and then they thought we must be rich and mean because they only got bread and marge and mixed fruit jam without any fruit in it, and my mother's rock cakes, that were rock-solid indeed, and perfectly smooth, like meteorites. No one ever came twice, but perhaps it wasn't only the rock cakes that put them off. Possibly they just didn't like us. I was all right, I think, but with the best will in the world you couldn't have called my sister Deborah likeable: no.

In fact we were not at all rich, quite the reverse. After my father died we stayed on in the too-large house where we were living at the time, and my mother went out to work to keep things going. This wasn't so much the done thing in those days, and Deborah and I hated coming home to the empty house, especially in winter when we knew that other people were coming home to nice fires and tea laid ready on the table. We detested it then, that house, as I built damp wigwams of paper and kindling in the cold hearth, while Deborah arranged meteorites on a plate and waited for the fire to catch so that she could make toast.

Eventually my mother decided that it might be a better bet to stay at home and take in lodgers or paying guests, and that was how we got Gil.

"What's the difference between a paying guest and a lodger?" Deborah asked.

"A lodger will just live here. A paying guest will live *with* us, as if she were family," my mother said. I'm not sure even now whether Gil was a paying guest or a lodger. I think he started as a lodger, but in the end we liked him so much that he was almost family anyway; almost we would have paid him to stay. It might be more accurate to say that in the end he wouldn't have stayed even if we had paid him.

I was fifteen that year, and Deborah was just coming up to twelve, so we were both at the same school again. We arrived home together one afternoon in May and found a young man on the doorstep, trying to make the bell ring. To be honest, we thought at first that it was a lady in trousers, until he turned round as we opened the gate. Deborah didn't hesitate to tell him so. She stood on the black and white tiled path and stared at him until he lost his nerve and looked at his feet.

"It's your hair," said Deborah.

"Oh," he said, as if he'd heard that one before. Long hair for men was only just becoming fashionable then, and hair like his we had never seen before. It was not only long, it was dark and thick, like very expensive fur, and it didn't just dangle limply over his shoulders, like pictures of Jesus. It encircled his head wholly, without a parting, as though it had a secret surging life of its own. It made me think, more than anything, of a well-tended piece of

74

topiary, springing from the slender, sturdy trunk of his neck.

"Do you live here?" he said at last, when he had looked up, found Deborah still gazing at him, and looked down again.

"Yes." I thought of our card in the glass case outside the post office. "Have you come about a room?"

"Is it still vacant?"

"At two pounds a week," Deborah said, quickly, "or three pounds ten shillings if we feed you, or five pounds if we treat you properly."

"Good God," he said. "How will you treat me for three pounds ten?"

I tried to explain, but Deborah got in first. "You'll get a smaller room, and you won't be able to have a bath every night, and you won't be part of the family."

He said, "What would I get for thirty bob? A mattress in the cellar and food lowered on a string?"

Just then my mother came in from the garden and saw us all through the glass panel in the front door. She rescued the young man from Deborah's basilisk eye and sent us to make tea. Deborah lit the gas under the kettle and tipped our kittens out of the tea cosy. I pummeled the bread to soften it up, and looked in the cake tin.

"Shall we give him meteorites?"

"It depends." Deborah took one and tapped it with a teaspoon. It shattered. "Do we want him to stay?"

Did we? I thought of seeing that wonderful hair across the table every day at breakfast and dinner. "Yes," I said firmly. "Don't you?"

"If he stops," said Deborah, "we could have proper

cakes, sometimes, and *butter*. We could travel on buses. No, not meteorites." She opened the bag of broken biscuits from Woolworth's and picked out the best ones, those with icing or only one corner missing. When we took the tea into the front room we discovered that he was going to stay and be treated fairly well for three pounds ten shillings a week.

"Not a paying guest, then," Deborah said severely. A paying guest would have meant a bus home from school, as well as going there, even if it wasn't raining.

"Will you be quiet, Deb?" my mother said. "Go and make up the bed if you want something to do. He's moving in tonight."

He was a painting student from the art college, and his name was Robin Gilbert, but everyone, he said, called him Gil, and so did we. Soon it was hard to believe that we had ever been without him. As well as paying for our butter and buses he was very good about carrying out the dustbin on Fridays, helping with the shopping, and cleaning the drains. For three pounds ten shillings he should have been doing his own washing, but soon his clothes appeared in the laundry basket with ours, by invitation.

"I don't see the point of him rinsing out his socks in the bathroom by night," said my mother, but it wasn't only socks.

"It's funny, seeing underpants on the line again," Deborah said, loudly, in the back garden, and all along the street you could see neighbors, who had been weeding, rear up and look over their hedges. They had taken to looking rather a lot, anyway, since Gil moved in with his hair. All the time he lived with us he never had it cut,

76

except at the end, and that wasn't exactly *cutting*. It seemed to grow thicker and longer as we watched, like mustard and cress on flannel.

In the mornings, when he joined us for breakfast, it was brushed smooth and seamless, so that looking over the landing banisters at him as he went downstairs, I was put in mind of a great dark glossy mushroom; but by evening, after a hard day in the studios—and he did work hard—it rolled and coiled about his head and shoulders in soft wild waves. Sometimes he came home with oil paint in it, and asked my mother for the loan of her scissors. She was horrified.

"You mustn't go hacking at it," she protested, and patiently sponged out the paint with cotton wool dipped in white spirit while he sat awkwardly, head bent, and doodled on the knee of his jeans with a ballpoint pen.

"I wouldn't miss an inch or two, here and there," Gil said.

"Vandalism," my mother said, teasing and combing. "If it were mine I wouldn't part with a millimeter." She couldn't keep her hands off that hair, none of us could. Any excuse was enough to set one of us patting, stroking, rearranging it; even Deborah, although she usually managed to snarl it up or get it wound painfully round a sleeve button.

"Wot, no dandruff?" said Deborah, rummaging through it like the nit nurse.

Poor, kind, long-suffering Gil: he wasn't at all vain, but he must have been proud of his hair or he would have trimmed it to a less tempting length and bought himself a bit of peace thereby. One afternoon, as he lay reading

77

on the lawn, the kittens got into it and had to be picked out, one claw at a time, like burrs.

Later that summer we acquired two real paying guests; my late father's killer aunt Jean, and her cousin Elsie. They moved into the big front bedroom for six weeks, and Great-Auntie Jean settled down to raise Cain for the duration. Cousin Elsie was popularly supposed to look after Great-Auntie Jean, but it was debatable. Cousin Elsie, at sixty-odd, wore little pink velvet bows in her hair and still bashed a hole in the bottom of her eggshells at breakfast in case the witches got hold of them and put to sea in search of hapless mariners.

" 'Oh, never leave your eggshells unbroken in the cup;
Think of us poor sailor-men and always smash them
   up,' "

chanted Cousin Elsie, pounding away with the handle of her spoon. She used to leave a little heap of uneaten food at the side of her plate for Mr. Manners. My mother, under stress, called her Barmy Elsie, but not to her face.

Gil, who had not gone home for the holidays but stayed with us in the city, to paint, was unfailingly kind to the old ladies, although to begin with we wouldn't have blamed him for fetching a hammer to Great-Auntie Jean. She took one look at his gleaming head and snapped, "I don't care for long hair on boys. It isn't manly."

Later: "*Is* it a boy?"

And later still: "He looks like the back end of a Pomeranian."

You could see where Deborah got it from.

But Gil just smiled and went on with the washing up,

78

also unmanly, until Great-Auntie Jean patted him on the head when he wasn't expecting it—causing him to jump and crack the milk jug against the cold tap—and said, "It's wasted on you, young man. Some gels would give a fortune to sprout a thatch like that."

Barmy Cousin Elsie was enchanted by Gil's hair. She seemed to forget that there was a human being underneath and petted it, when she could reach, chirruping as one does with small shy animals. Perhaps she hoped it would purr. Gil became rather nervous. I sometimes glimpsed on his face the look you see on Persian cats when they have been stroked once too often, especially if Deborah or Cousin Elsie were about; but after a time I noticed that he was beginning to look like that even when there was nobody about. I found him once, sitting on the back door-step and sketching the linear debris round the dustbin. For no apparent reason he stopped drawing very suddenly, his arm stiffened, then his shoulders. He bit hard into his lower lip, as if to stop himself from saying something he might regret later, and then whipped his head round so that his hair flew out like a dancer's tutu in a pirouette.

I never saw anyone look more dismayed than he did, when he found that there was no one behind him; but it happened again, more than once, and sometimes, stealth-ily, he would lift his hand and test the air at the back of his head, as if expecting to find another hand there. His expression, when Deborah and Cousin Elsie came close, was pitiable.

"Why don't you have it cut?" I asked, selflessly, for I could not bear to think of that rich harvest in wasted swathes on the beige linoleum round the barber's chair.

"Why—they won't stay for ever, will they?" he asked in an agonized whisper, glancing to where Great-Auntie Jean and Cousin Elsie wittered over tea cups in the front room.

"No, but it might make them keep their hands off till they go," I said, and without thinking I lifted my hand and gave his head a sympathetic pat.

He *cringed*.

Before the city reached out and put its arm around our house, it must have stood alone among fields. The other houses in the street were much newer and their gardens quite small. Ours was huge, with a kind of barn to one side where the car lived, when we had a car, and which was now used as a store for old furniture, jam jars, flowerpots and gardening tools, where rotted harness and perished hosepipes hung from a beam that ran from one side of the building to the other, fifteen feet above the ground. One August afternoon, while we were having a picnic tea on the lawn, Gil asked my mother if she would mind his using the barn to paint in.

"Of course not," she said. "It's a very good idea—if the roof doesn't leak. It would be a pity if your canvases were spoiled."

"I can fix the roof," Gil said, in a tight, miserable voice. I was surprised, expecting him to sound at least gratified by my mother's assent, but he looked even more hunted than usual. It was a very hot, utterly windless afternoon, but I observed that although Gil was prudently sitting well away from the rest of us, the hair at the back of his head was lifting and rippling as if someone were running it gently through her fingers. I could tell that it was all he

80

could do not to look over his shoulder, or raise his arm, but suddenly his head jerked back and he cried out, as much from fear as from pain, I thought.

"What is it?" my mother said, alarmed, and scrambled up to see if he were hurt. Gil saw her coming and took off across the lawn, his hand clapped to the back of his neck.

"Bee sting," he said, heading for the house. He kept turning round as he ran.

"Oh, how beastly," my mother cried, cantering after him. "Go into the kitchen; I'll put the blue-bag on it."

Up got Cousin Elsie, shrieking, "Vinegar! Vinegar! Vinegar for bees!"

"Vinegar for *wasps*," Great-Auntie Jean bellowed at their retreating backs. "Vinegar—wasps. V—W, that's how I remember. They come one after the other in the alphabet," she explained.

I left them to it and cleared away the tea things. I knew how it felt to have my hair pulled: nothing at all like a bee sting.

Gil had arranged to go to an exhibition in London with some friends, the next day, on the 7:50 train, but either he had forgotten to set his alarm clock or he had fallen asleep again after it rang, for at half-past seven he came slithering down the stairs in a panic, dragging a sweater over his head and with his boots in his hand. He hopped round the kitchen with a slice of toast between his teeth, trying to pull on the boots and dodge my mother who was pursuing him with a comb.

"I'm late," he said, at last, and the toast fell out of his mouth. It dropped into the cats' saucer.

"But Gil, your hair!" my mother said.

"I'll do it on the train." He retrieved the toast, larded with marmalade and Vitty-Kitty cat food, and ate it.

"But look at it. Whatever have you been doing?"

Gil paused on one leg, and glanced in the mirror over the sink. At first I'd thought his hair was simply tousled from sleep, but when he stopped gyrating I could see why my mother was so perturbed. His head was covered in plaits, dozens of tiny plaits that nestled among the unbraided hair like centipedes. A row of them swung in a fringe across his forehead, and one dangled in front of each ear like an Orthodox Jew's payess.

"It's the latest fashion," Deborah said. "He's doing his thing. Can I have Vitty-Kitty on *my* toast?"

"It doesn't suit you, Gil," my mother said. "Let me comb it out."

"All he needs now is a bunch of blue ribbons," said Great-Auntie Jean, spitefully leaving the quotation incomplete.

Gil seized the mirror and tried to see the back of his head in it. "I didn't do it," he said, when he could speak. "Who did this—I didn't!"

"It wasn't me," Deborah said, catching his eye in the mirror. "Don't look at me."

"Someone must have," Gil said. His voice was rising.

"Don't be silly," said my mother. "Who'd do that to you—?"

"D'you think I did it to *myself*?"

"—and how could they? You'd have *noticed*."

"Elf-locks," said Cousin Elsie, ramming the butter knife

through the bottom of her eggshell. "You must have of-
fended the little people."

"What the hell is she on about?" Gil shouted, white-
faced, white-lipped. He was trying to unravel the braided
strands but his hands were shaking and the little plaits
quivered in sympathy.

"Elf-locks," Cousin Elsie repeated, placidly. "If you
upset the fairies they steal into your room at night—through
the keyhole—and tie knots in your hair. You must have
been a very bad boy, Gil, to make them so thorough."

"Oh Jesus Christ," Gil said, through his teeth, and pushed
his way out of the kitchen. We heard him running upstairs
and then the bedroom door slammed shut. It was the first
time we had ever seen him lose his temper. He missed
the train. He didn't go to London.

"He must of done it in his sleep," Deborah said. "Must
of."

"He's working too hard," said my mother, fretfully.
"He imagines things." I suppose she was thinking of the
nonexistent bee sting which an exhaustive search had failed
to locate. Gil came down to lunch with his hair still slightly
crimped from the braiding, but that didn't explain why
one strand, over his left temple, should keep curling up
and uncoiling, as if it were being wound round somebody's
finger. Gil ate very little. He said it was the after-effects
of Vitty-Kitty and marmalade.

Following this incident he spent more and more time
in the barn, working at his canvases. My mother was more
than ever convinced that he was working too hard, and
certainly he had become very pale and hollow-eyed. He

kept several paintings on the go at once; one on his easel and the others ranged round the walls. On the night before the autumn term began he stayed out there very late, packing up his finished work to take back to college with him. I had gone to bed before he came in, and the next morning he overslept. When half-past eight struck, and no Gil, my mother became concerned.

"Take him up some tea," she said, handing me a cup with the saucer on top in case it was slopped in transit. I knocked on Gil's door. There was a sound inside that might have been "Come in" and might not. I turned the handle anyway and opened the door.

It was dark in there, the curtains still drawn. The bed was on the far side of the room and I could just see his hair spread out on the pillow, but he didn't raise his head, or even a hand.

"It's half-past eight," I said. "You'll be late . . . Gil? Gil, are you all right?"

"Who is it?" he said. "Dinah?"

"Yes. What's wrong?"

"Come over here and shut the door."

I didn't quite like to be in his room with him in it, but I did as he said. I could tell there was something wrong by his voice. He lay quite still as I put the saucer on the bedside table and the cup on the saucer, but by the disordered bedclothes I could see that he must have been thrashing about before I came in.

He said, "Something's happened to my head. I can't move my head."

"You've got a stiff neck?"

84

"No—it's not like that—I just can't move it. Can you see anything?"

It didn't look as if there was anything *to* see, but I leaned across the bed and opened the curtains. "Does it hurt?" I turned to face him, rather shy about seeing him in bed, especially when I noticed that he slept without a pajama jacket which I thought, then, rather daring. He was lying in a very strange position, on his side, with one arm braced against the edge of the bed as if he were trying to lever himself up, but with his head buried in the pillow; I should say, rather, *forced* into it. His hair lay round his face like deep shadow. He looked terribly frightened.

"Does it hurt?" I said again. I was afraid to touch him. "Did you strain it last night?"

"Strain my head?"

"Your neck."

"It's not my neck." He turned his eyes upwards, not to me, but toward the bed's head. *"Something's leaning on my hair."*

"Nothing's leaning on your hair," I said. We were both whispering; I don't know why. "How could it be?" But when I looked more closely I saw that his hair was oddly flattened against the linen, like grass when the wind blows on it.

"I don't know—I don't know what," he said. "Make it go away, get it off me, oh Dinah, get it off."

"But there's nothing there. Can't you see there's nothing there?"

"Then move the pillow!" I could see what he meant. I would be like whipping away a chair as someone sat down.

85

I took hold of the pillow case and yanked it towards me. The bedside table went over and so did I, for the pillow, when it came, did not come easily. There seemed to be a fearful weight upon it, a weight far greater than even the heaviest head of hair. At the same moment Gil rolled off the bed and on to the carpet, where he sprawled on his back among the twisted bedding like a merman washed up on the beach after a storm.

I sat up, hurriedly. "Gil, what was it?"

"I don't know," he said. He wrapped his arms round his head, enfolding all his hair, and cradled it possessively. "It was a stiff neck. It must have been a stiff neck." I went to fetch him some more tea. "It *must* have been," he said, when I came back. "Mustn't it? Don't say anything, please. Don't tell anyone." I didn't intend to tell anyone.

He was back at college for the rest of that week, and now had evening classes too, so he missed all the fun of Great-Auntie Jean and Cousin Elsie moving out and going home to hibernate in Harrogate. My mother and Deborah and I celebrated having the house to ourselves once more (for of course, by now, we counted Gil as one of ourselves) in spite of our reduced circumstances, but on Saturday Deborah was sent out to insert another card in the glass case outside the post office. I was hanging out the washing when she came back, and Gil was working in the barn where he had been since before breakfast, in spite of his disturbed night. He had roused us all at three in the morning by rushing out on to the landing shouting, "Get out! Get out! Get out of my hair!" Hideously embarrassed, he had apologized and said it was a nightmare. Deborah and

I went across to the barn to see how he was feeling, as much out of kindness as curiosity.

Gil had abandoned his painting and was standing in the middle of the floor, looking up at the traverse beam. His head was tilted right back, and his hair fell half down to his waist. I caught Deborah's hand just as she was reaching out to touch it. He turned round and pointed to the beam.

"Look at that. How on earth did it get up there?"

Halfway along the beam was one of our kittens, now nearly a full-grown cat, but still inefficient. The only way to reach the beam was by climbing a vertical row of iron spikes driven into the wall; clever kitty had gone up the spikes and along the beam where she now sat marooned with flattened ears and gaping mouth: "Meeow, meeow, meeow."

"I'll go," Deborah said. Deborah was renowned at school for her gymnastic skill, among other things, but Gil didn't know that. He looked at the beam, and the spikes, and said, "No, it's too dangerous. I'll get her down."

He didn't have any trouble climbing up to the beam, but when he reached it he crouched against the sloping roof and said doubtfully, "It's narrower than I thought."

"Then let *me*," Deborah said, not realizing that he had been gallant and imagining that he was trying to steal her thunder. "I'm thinner than you."

This was so, but only just. Gil shook his head and moved away from the spikes. At first he crawled along the beam, but as he reached the middle, and the kitten, he lay down flat and stretched out one arm.

"Come on, kitty; good kitty; kitty-kitty-kitty."

The kitten advanced trustfully and then, pausing only

to toy with a tendril of hair, walked past his hand, over his head, along his back, and proceeded to the end of the beam above the spikes, where it sat down and began to yell again.

"Wouldn't you just know it?" Gil asked, of no one in particular, and started to edge backwards along the beam, inch by inch. Then he stopped, and said very quietly, *"My hair."*

"What about your rotten hair?" Deborah asked, coldly. She had swarmed up the spikes to fetch the kitten, hell-bent on cornering some of the glory.

"It's caught on something." He was clinging to the beam for dear life, literally for dear life, and tugging his head sideways in frantic, terrified jerks. "I can't move. I can't move, Dinah, it's got me again." And then he cried out, not to me, "Let go! Let me go! *Let go of my hair!*" and forgetting where he was, I suppose, in his panic, he struck out with both hands, and slipped.

He seemed to roll over dreadfully slowly, and I ran forward with the ridiculous idea of catching him as he fell, but he hadn't fallen; didn't fall. He was still above me, hanging above me, hanging from the beam by his hair. His head was dragged back against the wood, face up, so that where I stood I could see only his jaw, his voiceless, arching, gasping throat and the taut, straining hair, while he clawed and kicked at everything, at nothing, and flung wide his imploring arms, crucified on . . . nothing.

I called up at him, "Hang on, Gil, hang on," but he couldn't hang on and he couldn't fall, and I heard Deborah's still small voice in my ear, saying, "That must be what happened to Absalom."

I had forgotten about Deborah, until she spoke. She had climbed down the spikes with the kitten and, shoving past me in her haste, was now rooting among the rubbish at the end of the barn. "Deb, get a ladder. Tell someone, fetch someone, oh, run, Deb, run!"

Deborah was running, all right, back to the spikes and up them; and in her free hand she carried the axe that my father had once used to chop firewood. Balancing as elegantly as she did in the gym at school, she stepped out along the beam, halted one pace away from Gil's paralyzed head, and raised the axe.

He screamed. I'd never heard a man scream before, but I didn't think any the less of him for it. I screamed too when Deborah brought down the axe in one clean stroke, to sever the hair that bound him there.

It was, as I said, a fifteen-foot drop, and I like to think that in the heat of the moment Deborah simply forgot what the consequences of her action were likely to be. Gil broke his leg and his collar bone but, all things considered, he was lucky not to break his neck. In any case, he was out cold, whether from fright or concussion I don't know, and in no condition to detail his injuries before the ambulance arrived and took him to hospital. My mother went with him, under the impression that he had risked his life in a foolhardy but laudable attempt to save our cretinous kitty. In the excitement it escaped her attention that Gil had finally had his hair cut, and she failed to notice Father's axe, buried deep in the beam, and as soon as the ambulance had driven away Deborah went back up the spikes to retrieve it. I stayed on the ground, still shaken and sick, and could not look as she cavorted overhead, but I called out, "Deb, bring down his hair," thinking: If he dies, I shall have it to remember him by. Fortunately he did not die, for I didn't get it.

"What hair?" Deborah said.

"For crying out loud, Deb, you cut through his hair, didn't you?"

"He thought I was going to cut off his head," Deborah remarked, complacently. "I could see it in his eyes. That's why he screamed." It occurred to me then that she would cherish that moment for the rest of her life.

"But where's all his hair?"

"On his head, I suppose. There's none here."

"There must be, it was caught up on something, wasn't it? That's what made him slip. That's what held him up."

"No, it wasn't." Deborah squatted on the beam and looked down at me between her knees like a gibbon in a tree. "It wasn't caught up on anything. It was all bunched together and pulled tight round the beam, but it wasn't caught. It looked more like someone was holding it, to me." She paused. "Someone *was* holding it."

"Then where is it? The bit you cut off? There must have been so much." I looked all round, on the floor. "It's not down here."

"It's not up here, either," Deborah said, and it wasn't. It wasn't anywhere. Whoever it was who had loved Gil's beautiful hair so much, more even than we did, had got what she wanted. I hoped that, having got what she wanted, she would let him alone when he came back, but, not surprisingly, he never did come back.

Aidan Chambers

Room 18

I arrived in Dublin late one night. The boat from Holyhead had been unusually full and the crossing one of the roughest in living memory. The Irish Sea had done its worst: every soul aboard had been wretchedly sick, and we docked four hours late.

Clearing customs was more tiresome than ever. The sight of all those bilious faces, and the sour smell of sickness that hung about us as we crowded the customs shed affected even the poker-faced officers. They passed us through as quickly as a respectable show of authority would allow.

I jumped in a taxi as soon as I could, and gave the name of my usual hotel.

"You'll have trouble if you're not booked," the driver said as I sat back in my seat.

"I never have before," I replied, though not without

apprehension. Taxi drivers make a habit of pessimism; but they also know what's on about town.

"And maybe you've never been in Dublin during the Festival time?"

"The Festival!"

" 'Tis plays and poetry and moving pictures, and all making on they are Irish, though most of it comes from England and America," the driver said and laughed.

I realized then why the boat had been so crowded, and cursed myself for letting business preoccupations blind me to the doings of the rest of the world.

We drew up outside the hotel. People thronged the entrance.

"Will you wait, in case they are full?" I asked the driver.

He snugged his cloth cap and glanced over his shoulder. "It's a very good night for work," he said. "The Festival does bring in the trade, I will say that. It does indeed."

I handed him a pound note.

"I'll wait, sir," he said, "seeing you're likely to be in such difficulties!"

Before I reached the hotel door, a commissionaire barred my way as though staving off a platoon of attacking Black and Tans.

"Would you be wanting a room, sir?" he asked.

I nodded.

"Not a hope of even a chair in the lobby tonight," he said.

I got back into the taxi.

"Why sure that was mighty bad luck," said the driver brightly. "I felt in my bones you might just be in time."

"Now where?" I said, too weary and depressed to give much thought to the answer.

"That," said the driver pointedly, "is a mighty problematical question!"

The Irish Sea doing its worst had left me in no mood for Irish riddles. All I wanted was a bed for the night, and I could not have cared less at that moment where it was. Later on I was to care a good deal. I took another note from my wallet and passed it to the driver. He accepted it without a word, slipped into gear, and headed up O'Connell Street.

We drew up outside an ill-lit, ill-kempt Victorian building in a side street well away from the center of town. It was hardly the kind of place I would normally have looked at twice, never mind asked for a room.

"I'm not promisin' anything, you understand," the driver said, "but if they've nothing else at all, I'll lay a small wager you'll find room 18 free."

"Room 18?"

"That'll be a couple of quid on the clock, and if you don't mind, I'll not wait. My time's up for this day, and I'm more pleased than sorry about that."

I paid the fare, climbed out, and watched the taxi accelerate away as though it was my last lifeline to civilization. In the glimmer of the back-street lamps the hotel looked even gloomier than it had from inside the taxi. The downstairs rooms were dark, and only one or two windows in the upper stories were lighted. There were none of the refinements of smarter places: no bright neon signs, no canopied entrance, no commissionaires to push open the doors.

Inside, the lobby was more a passageway than a hall. The carpet was worn, and an unshaded bulb, the only source of light, hung from the ceiling above the reception desk, a mahogany affair, heavy and finger-marked like a bar in a seedy public house.

There was an old-fashioned brass handbell on the desk by the registration book, and as no one seemed to be about, I struck it. It clanged unexpectedly loud. After a moment an old chap came from a room behind the counter. His aged face was shaped so like the map of his native land, I almost laughed.

He said nothing, merely inclined the map of Ireland towards me with the kind of annoyed look people wear when they have been woken unnecessarily from a nap.

"Have you a room?" I asked, and even my anxiety to get some rest could not hide the irritation in my voice.

"In Festival time?" said the map, speaking from somewhere in the region of County Limerick.

"Nothing at all?"

A shake of the head.

"What about room 18?"

I had not expected quite the reaction I got. The old fellow's body braced, his eyebrows shot up. He stared at me with peculiar interest.

"It's not a room we usually let," he said.

Had I not been so weary, I might have asked why. But weariness kills curiosity about everything but the means of rest.

"If you have it available, I'll be glad to take it," I said. "I've had a rough crossing from England, and Dublin, as

94

you know, is crowded. I'll settle for anything that has a bed in it."

The old chap looked a me a moment. Then he said:

"You're either exhausted, or mad, or maybe both. And then again, you might just be more brass-faced than most of your nation. But whatever it is, I'll tell you what I'll do. Pay your board for the night on the nail, and in cash, and the room is yours."

I took out my wallet. "You're not very trusting," I said.

" 'Tisn't that I don't trust you," he said, smiling. " 'Tis just the thought came to me that you might be leavin' early."

"I doubt if I shall," I said. "I'm much too tired for early rising."

"Remains to be seen," he muttered, and took the money.

The old man led me to a room on the second floor. It was at the end of a corridor, and I judged it to be at the side of the building. There, he handed me the key, without opening the door, looked at me as one might look at someone about to embark on a dangerous journey, nodded good-night, and shuffled off down the dingy passage. I could not help thinking how his slight frame and wild white hair made him look like a retreating leprechaun.

I unlocked the door and went into the room.

At this point I should say that I am not by nature either nervous or easily frightened. I do not believe in things supernatural, and have never found need for the comforts of religion. I am a scientist and a businessman, and known for my hardness of head and coolness of nerve in tight situations. All I can say is that my experiences in this room

95

and afterwards certainly happened. Further than that I won't go. I have never tried to explain them to myself, nor to anyone else.

The air inside the room smelt dank and musty, and so, while I unpacked, I put my wristwatch between the sheets of the bed. When I took it out, the glass was steamed up. I had learned the trick long ago as a traveling consultant, an occupation that took me round the world and into all kinds of hotel bedrooms. It was a sure way of discovering whether a bed was damp. This one certainly was: it had not been aired or slept in for weeks.

Resigned to the worst—I was too tired to waste time getting it dried out—I climbed into bed. A faint unease had settled over me since entering the room, and so for a moment as I lay there, I looked about.

There was nothing in the room that led me then to expect what happened later. A bulky and extremely ugly wardrobe stood to one side of the door, taking up what remained of the wall on that side. An ornate nineteenth-century fireplace with dull brass attachments almost covered the wall opposite the bed. The large gilt-framed looking-glass above the fireplace was pockmarked with damp, as though huge flies had blown on it. In the wall opposite the wardrobe and to my right as I lay in bed was a narrow sash window with heavy undrawn drapes hanging at either side. Beneath it stood a curious wooden chest, about six feet long and three deep, with a lid that opened upwards. Had I been less tired, I might have opened the chest and looked inside; but nothing else in the room excited even the mildest curiosity, and now that the bed was growing warm enough to bring the first drowsiness of sleep, I was only too ready to switch off the light and give myself up to it.

I woke suddenly, in a heavy sweat. The room was oppressively hot, with a dry burning heat like that from an electric fire. My face felt flushed, and the skin tingled. The wetness of my body might have been due to the dampness of the bed, but the temperature of the room I could not explain: it was a cold night outside, and the room was unheated.

I sat up, intending to throw off some bed-clothes. But as I pulled the top coverings from me, I realized that, though there was no light in the room nor any coming in from outside, I could clearly see the clothes on the bed.

I looked round. The entire room was lit by a strange luminosity, a brightness that could come from neither sun nor moon, nor any man-made source. Every object in the room was visible, not from any light shining *on* it, but from its own incandescence. Each object glowed, as the hands of a luminous watch glow in the dark, possessing the source of light themselves. It was a greenish glister that left the walls and all the air in the room as black as impenetrable night. Half awake, I stared with puzzled incomprehension at the bed and wardrobe, the fireplace, the frame of the looking-glass, and the curious oblong box. Each one radiated the unearthly light.

I told myself it was an optical illusion, a trick of light caused, perhaps, by something I could not see outside the window.

But then something moved in the mirror. Instinctively, I looked across at it. Though the frame round the glass glowed eerily, the glass itself was dark. Dark, that is, except for the pockmarks of damp. These were visible, glowing less brightly than the objects in the room, as if they alone might be reflecting some of the green glister. And it was these spots that were moving.

I now became wide awake, sitting tense in the bed, sweating more than ever. The spots moved at first in no discernible pattern. But the movement did not seem to be without aim or purpose; rather, I felt, each point of light was *being moved*. It was as though some invisible hand guided the lights about, like pieces in a jigsaw, searching for the place into which each piece must fit. I watched, fascinated; and as I watched, the speed at which the spots were moved increased; and as the speed increased, the spots closed together, combining, adding themselves one to another, until at last there *was* a shape, a pattern I could recognize. The shape was vague at first, without details. But these were added: some lights in the pattern dimmed, others brightened, until gradually the flat, one-dimensional pattern took on form and depth, shadows and highlights.

I caught my breath, aghast at what I saw. For the form that appeared was the face of a man.

The face was caught as it might have been in a photograph—I can find no other way to describe it—not the printed positive, but the negative of a photograph: all the darks and lights reversed. Thus the irises of the eyes glowed, the whites were black, the shadows round the deep-sunk eyes shone. And the eyes were turned on me.

A cry rose in me, a cry like those that break one from a nightmare too horrible to dream. The cry rose, but could not find voice. The oppressive heat seemed to hold me by the throat, so that the cry was strangled there, and all that escaped was a stifled, low-toned groan. Though I wished to take my eyes from the face watching me from the mirror, I could not; while every second the image grew brighter, more clearly defined, till it blazed there, a more brilliant glare than any in the room.

As I gazed, the knowledge came to me that in some unthinkable way my presence in this room had set free forces that were bringing me to the very barrier between life and death; that what I now saw formed on the surface of the mirror was the image of death. Life and death are, after all, merely reflections of something greater, more powerful than both. I do not believe in God; but that there is a force, an energy that transcends the life we know, I have no doubt. And in those confused and horrified moments, I could think only one thing: that the image on the mirror, reversed from what it would have been in life, was a sudden glimpse of death.

I have said that the image was fixed, as in a photograph. So it was, at first. Once fully formed, however, strengthened in shape and brightness, it began to move. The eyes stayed on mine, but the head nodded as if replying to my racing thoughts with an unspoken "Yes."

What little calm of reason I had left told me one thing: I must at all costs prevent the image from holding my attention. I must break myself from it. Why I should have felt that the image had a will, and that it meant to crush my own and overpower me, I do not know. But I felt this most strongly. I tried to turn my mind to other things, daily things, dreary things, anything to distract me. That ghastly crossing of the Irish Sea; the crowded Dublin streets; tomorrow's business appointment.

Sure enough, as I forced these mundane thoughts upon myself, the brilliance of the face began to fade. Encouraged by my success, I sought other topics that might rid me altogether of the awful image.

I thought of the taxi driver. The image faded more.

I thought of the bribes he had taken. The brightness dimmed again.

But thinking of the taxi driver brought another thought. How had he known about this room? How could he know it would be free?

No sooner had the questions come to me than the image brightened at once.

"Oh, no!" I tried to shout, and could not. Desperately, I pushed the thought from my mind and croaked aloud the first words that came into my head.

"The square on the hypotenuse is equal to the sum of the squares on the other two sides."

The image dimmed a little.

"I am John Randolph Taylor, of Cheyne Walk, Birmingham, England, and I have one wife, two sons, and a baby daughter."

The image faded more.

But whose is the face on the mirror?

The image brightened.

The question had slipped into my head unplanned, unwished for. But it came so strongly that it seemed to shout itself inside my brain. I struggled against it.

"I am an electronics engineer, and do not believe in the supernatural."

And who are you?

"I play golf on Sundays and whenever I can find the time."

And who are you?

"My favorite meal is lobster salad."

And who are you?

"I am forty-three and suffer from nothing but occasional indigestion."

But who are you? Who? Who?

Nothing I could do erased that question. It possessed me, fascinated me. Who was this man whose image was linked in some way to myself? Deep within me, perverse and undeniable, was the desire to know the answer, no matter how appalling the horror that might attend it. Instinctively, I knew that to speak the thought aloud might release forces terrible and overwhelming, and leave me with no hope of ridding myself of the image on the mirror. Instinctively I knew this, and so drew back; only to find myself mocking my lack of courage, my weakness: urging myself to pit my disbelief of the supernatural against the fact of what my eyes could see.

At that moment the constriction in my throat eased, and I shouted firmly: "Who are you?"

I had not finished the words before the green image blazed like a protracted flash of forked lightning. The room shook, the multitude of gleaming spots broke from the mirror like sparks from an electrode. For some minutes they crackled round the room, chaotic and dazzling. Then, almost as if they had been signaled, they streamed towards a point between the bed and the fireplace, and gathered. The form they took was unshaped, a pillar of sparkling lights, each no bigger than a pinhead.

Now the light in the furniture began to shimmer; the outline blurred; and then, like iron filings to a magnet, the luminosity from each object flowed towards the pillar and was absorbed by it, until the furniture was drained of light, and darkness was everywhere in the room, except for the blazing pillar of moving particles standing man-high at the foot of my bed.

It hovered there, and yet to say it was anywhere is not to speak the truth. There are no words that can tell what I saw and felt. The pillar was before my eyes; but I knew that, if I tried to touch it, my hands would pass through, feeling nothing. It was visible, but had no substance. I *saw* it before me, but I *felt* enclosed by it. Nor can I tell how long this lasted. Time, like space, meant nothing now: it was endless, yet no longer than it takes to blink an eye.

Like a branch spreading from a tree trunk, a limb—no, not a limb; merely a part of it—came reaching out from the pillar towards me. I would have moved, but could not. Had hoops of steel bound me, I could not have been held more rigid. I could only sit and watch the limb of bright sparks reach out to me, pass over my face, play over my body, enfold me in green light. I felt no physical pain, no burning or piercing, no sense of being touched. But the very instant the first of those flecks of light reached me, the energy in my body began to drain away. If I were a religious man, I would say my very soul was being sucked from deep within me. But I can take no such view. All I know is that the power that makes men active, living beings—the essence of life itself—was being transfused from me by that mobile limb. And at once the pillar of light, with seeming pain and difficulty, changed into a vague, but recognizable, human figure.

Slowly the figure developed, features were moulded, again as in a photograph, though not now as a negative but as a positive; a positive printed in shimmering electric green.

When at last the limb withdrew and became itself an arm of the newborn figure, I knew the answer to the question I had shouted endless moments ago. And now a cry did break from me, for what I saw was terrifying and awful, worse—much worse—than any dream or nightmare could ever be. What I saw was a man, and that man was no stranger. He was myself.

True, he was older than I. His hair was balding, and mine—then—was thick. His face was lined with worry and pain, and mine—then—was smooth. But I knew him at once. He was myself—myself as I would be in years to come.

Even as I cried out, the specter came towards me. Slowly. Neither walking nor moving round the bed. But straight at me it came. And as it came, it took the shape of my own fear-bristled body as I lay in the bed.

I struggled to escape the advancing figure, pushing myself up in the bed, till I was pressed against the headboard and could go no farther. There I cowered in an agony of terror. And every slightest movement of my own body I saw reflected in the body of the specter; while the face of the advancing image showed me myself in all the ugliness of panic and fear: contorted, wild-eyed, the mouth open in a hysterical scream.

The form came within inches of my own. And suddenly

103

I knew that above all I must prevent that other self from fusing with me: knew that this was exactly what it meant to do. I must not let that precisely similar shape meet mine, absorb me, become superimposed upon me. For that would be to join life and death, to know more than any man can know, and live.

Again I cried out loud. But this was no cry of terror: it was the roar of a man summoning up every ounce of strength he has left in a last desperate battle for survival.

That very moment, the image reached me. My body was charged as if by a massive electric shock. Violent shudders racked me. The entire room shook, and I heard a noise like that of rushing wind. I flung myself about the bed, determined to resist the fusing of the image with myself. I kicked, I thrashed my arms, I curled and uncurled my body. The heat became intense. I felt as though I wrestled with a scorching ball of fire. My heart raced and pounded, my lungs strained till I thought they must burst. And with a last supreme effort of body and will, I hurled myself from the bed.

The multitude of dazzling points of light that formed the specter exploded wildly about the room. There was a loud noise of explosion. I was thrown against the wall so hard the breath was crushed from me.

I fell to the floor and lost consciousness.

The first light of dawn was streaming through the window when I came to, lying as I had fallen, my body stiff and painful. I stood up, trembling and groaning. Apart from the rumpled bed, everything was as it had been the night before. At first I was dazed, but gradually all that had happened came back to mind. And as it came, it brought one desire: to be gone from that hideous room.

I dressed with as much speed as my aching bones would allow, took my bags, and left without seeing anyone. The last thing I looked at in the room was the mirror above the fireplace. The pockmarks were there, as formless as when I had first noticed them.

Years have passed since that time, and in those years the horror of room 18 has dimmed. Sometimes, to entertain friends, I have told the tale, passing it off as an amusing, half-imagined party piece. Today, however, I was in my bedroom dressing for a dinner engagement. As I stood before the mirror attempting to get my tie straight, it struck me how like the face in that nightmare room my own had become. But what has caused me far more alarm is what I saw just behind the glass of the mirror.

There, newly formed, were a few tiny spots, like pockmarks of damp.

Joan Aiken

Old Fillikin

Miss Evans, the math teacher, had thick white skin, pocked like a nutmeg grater; her lips were pale and thick, often puffed out with annoyance; her thick hair was the drab color of old straw that has gone musty; and her eyes, behind thick glass lenses, stared angrily at Timothy.

"Timothy, how often have I *told* you," she said. "You have *got* to show your working. Even if these were the right answers—which they are not—I should give you no marks for them, because no working is shown. How, may I ask, did you arrive at this answer?"

Her felt-tip pen made two angry red circles on the page. All Timothy's neat layout—and the problems were tidily and beautifully set out, at least—all that neat arrangement had been spoiled by a forest of furious red X's, underlinings, and crossings-out, that went from top to bottom of the page, with a big W for Wrong beside each answer. The page was horrible now—like a scarred face, like a wrecked garden—Timothy could hardly bear to look at it.

"Well? How did you get that answer? Do you *understand* what I'm asking you?"

The trouble was that when she asked him a sharp question like that, in her flat, loud voice, with its aggressive north-country vowels—*an*swer, *ask*, with a short *a* as in grab or bash—he felt as if she were hammering little sharp nails into his brain, at once all his wits completely deserted him, the inside of his head was a blank numbness, empty and echoing like a hollow pot, as if his intelligence had escaped through the holes she had hammered.

"I don't know," he faltered.

"You *don't know*? How can you not *know*? You must have got those answers *some*how! Or do you just put down any figures that come into your head? If you'd got them *right*, I'd assume you'd copied the answers from somebody else's book—but it's quite plain you didn't do that—"

She stared at him in frustrated annoyance, her eyes pinpointed like screw tips behind the thick glass.

Of course he would not be such a fool as to copy someone else's book. He hardly ever got a sum right. If he had a whole series correct, it would be grounds for instant suspicion.

"Well, as you have this whole set wrong—plainly you haven't grasped the principle at all—I'll just have to set you a new lot. Here—you can start at the beginning of chapter VIII, page 64, and go as far as page 70."

His heart sank horribly. They were all the same kind—the kind he particularly hated—pages and pages of them. It would take him the whole weekend—and now, late on

Friday evening—for she had kept him after class—he was already losing precious time.

"Do you understand? Are you following me? I'd better explain the principle again."

And she was off, explaining; her gravelly voice went on and on, about brackets, bases, logarithms, sines, cosines, goodness knows what, but now, thank heaven, his mind was set free, she was not asking questions, and so he could let his thoughts sail off on a string, like a kite flying higher and higher . . .

"Well?" she snapped. "Have you got it now?"

"Yes—I think so."

"What have I been saying?"

He looked at her dumbly.

But just then a merciful bell began to ring, for the boarders' supper.

"I've got to go," he gasped, "or I'll miss my bus."

Miss Evans unwillingly gave in.

"Oh, very well. Run along. But you'll *have* to learn this, you know—you'll never pass exams, never get *any*-where, unless you do. Even farmers need math. Don't think *I* enjoy trying to force it into your thick head—it's no pleasure to *me* to have to spend time going over it all again and again—"

He was gathering his books together—the fat, ink-stained grey textbook, the glossy blue new one, the rough note-book, the green exercise book filled with angry red corrections—horrible things, he loathed the very sight and feel of them. If only he could throw them down the well, burn them, never open them again. Some day he would be free of them.

He hurried out, ran down the steps, tore across the school courtyard. The bus was still waiting beyond the gate; with immense relief he bounded into it and flung himself down on the prickly moquette seat.

If only he could blot Miss Evans and the hateful math out of his mind for two days; if only he could sit out under the big walnut tree in the orchard, and just draw and draw and let his mind fly like a kite, and think of nothing at all but what picture was going to take shape under his pencil, and in what colors, later, he would paint it; but now that plan was spoiled, he would have to work at those horrible problems for hours and hours, with his mind jammed among them, like a mouse caught in some diabolical machinery that it didn't invent, and doesn't begin to understand.

The bus stopped at a corner by a bridge, and he got out, climbed a fence, and walked across fields to get to the farm where he lived. There was a way round by a cart track, the way the postman came, but it took longer. The fields smelt of warm hay, and the farmyard of dry earth, and cattle-cake, and milk, and tractor-oil; a rooster crowed in the orchard, and some ducks quacked close at hand; all these were homely, comforting, familiar things, but now they had no power to comfort him; they were like helpless friends holding out their hands to him as he was dragged away to prison.

"These are *rules*, can't you see?" Miss Evans had stormed at him. "You have to learn them."

"Why?" he wanted to ask. "Who made those rules? How can you be certain they were right? Why do you turn upside down and multiply? Why isn't there any square root of minus one?"

109

But he never had the courage to ask that kind of question.

Next morning he went out and sat with his books in the orchard, under the big walnut, by the old well. It would have been easier to concentrate indoors, to work on the kitchen table, but the weather was so warm and still that he couldn't bear not to be out of doors. Soon the frosts would begin; already the walnut leaves, yellow as butter, were starting to drift down, and the squashy walnut rinds littered the dry grass and stained his bare feet brown; the nights were drawing in.

For some reason he remembered a hymn his granny used to say to him:

> Every morning the red sun
> Rises warm and bright,
> But the evening soon comes on
> And the dark cold night.

The words frightened him, he could not say why.

He tried to buckle his mind to his work. "If $r \geqq 4$, r weighings can deal with $2^r - 1$ loads—" but his thoughts trickled away like a river in sand. He had been dreaming about his grandmother—who died two years ago. In his dream they had been here, in the orchard, but it was winter, thick grey frost all over the grass, a fur of frost on every branch and twig and grass blade. Granny had come out of the house with her old zinc pail to get water from the well. "Tap water's no good to you," she always used to say. "Never drink water that's passed through metal pipes, it'll line your innards with tin, you'll end up clinking like a moneybox. Besides, tap water's full of those floorides and kloorides and wrigglers they put in it (letting

110

on as it's for your good—hah!); I'd not pay a penny for a hundred gallons of the stuff. Well water's served me all my life long, and it'll go on doing. Got some taste to it—not like that nasty flat stuff."

"I'll wind up the bucket for you, Granny," he said, and took hold of the heavy well handle.

"That's me boy! One hundred and eight turns."

"A hundred and eight is nine twelves. Nine tens are ninety, nine elevens are ninety-nine, nine twelves are a hundred and eight."

"Only in your book, lovie. In mine it's different. We have different ones!"

An ironic smile curved her mouth, she stood with arms folded over her clean blue-and-white print overall while he wound and counted. Eighty-nine, ninety, ninety-one, ninety-two—

When he had the dripping, double-cone-shaped well bucket at the top, and was going to tilt it, so as to fill her small pail, she had exclaimed, "Well, look who's come up with it! Old Fillikin!"

And that, for some reason, had frightened him so much that he had not dared look into the bucket but dropped it so that it went clattering back into the well and he woke up.

This seemed odd, remembering the dream in daylight, for he had loved his grandmother dearly. His own mother had died when he was two, and Granny had always looked after him. She had been kind, impatient, talkative, always ready with an apple, a hug, a slice of bread-and-dripping if he was hungry or hurt himself. She was full of unexpected ideas and odd information.

111

"Husterloo's the wood where Reynard the fox keeps his treasure. If we could find that, *I* could stop knitting, and *you* could stop thinking. You think too much, for a boy your age.

"The letter N is a wriggling eel. His name is No one, and his number is Nine.

"Kings always die standing up, and that's the way I mean to die."

She had, too, standing in the doorway, shouting after the postman, "If you don't bring me a letter tomorrow, I'll write your name on a leaf, and shut it in a drawer!"

Some people had thought she was a witch, because she talked to herself such a lot, but Timothy found nothing strange about her; he had never been in the least frightened of her.

"Who were you talking to, Granny?" he would say, if he came into the kitchen when she was rattling off one of her monologues.

"I was talking to Old Fillikin," she always answered, just as, when he asked, "What's for dinner, Granny?" she invariably said, "Surprise pie with pickled questions."

"Who's Old Fillikin?" he asked once, and she said, "Old Fillikin's my friend. My familiar friend. Every man has a friend in his sleeve."

"Have I got one, Granny?"

"Of course you have, love. Draw his picture, call him by his name, and he'll come out."

Now, sitting by the well, in the warm, hazy sunshine, Timothy began to wonder what Old Fillikin, Granny's familiar friend, would have looked like, if he had existed. The idea was, for some reason, not quite comfortable, and he tried to turn his mind back to his math problems.

"R weighings can deal with $2^r - 1$ loads . . ." but somehow the image of Old Fillikin would keep sneaking back among his thoughts, and, almost without noticing that he did so, he began to doodle in his rough notebook.

Old Fillikin fairly leapt out of the page: every stroke, every touch of the point, filled him in more swiftly and definitely. Old Fillikin was a kind of hairy frog; he looked soft and squashy to the touch—like a rotten pear, or a damp eiderdown—but he had claws too, and a mouthful of needle-sharp teeth. His eyes were very shrewd—they were a bit like Granny's eyes; but there was a sad, lost look about them too, as there had been about Granny's; as if she were used to being misunderstood. Old Fillikin was not a creature that you would want to meet in a narrow high-banked lane, with dusk falling. At first Timothy was not certain of his size. Was he as big as an apple, so that he could float, bobbing, in a bucket drawn up from a well, or was he, perhaps, about the size of Bella the Tamworth sow? The pencil answered that question, sketching in a gate behind Old Fillikin, which showed that he was at least two feet high.

"Ugh!" said Timothy, quite upset at his own creation, and he tore out the page from his notebook, scrumpled it up, and dropped it down the well.

$$\frac{dy}{dx} = \lim_{dx \to 0} \frac{f(x + dx) - f(x)}{dx}$$

"*Numbers!*" he remembered Granny scoffing, years ago, when he was hopelessly bogged down in his seven-times table. "Some people think they can manage everything

113

by numbers. As if they were set in the ground like bricks!"

"How do you mean, Granny?"

"As if you daren't slip through between!"

"But how *can* you slip between them, Granny? There's nothing between one and two—except one-and-a-half."

"You think there's only one lot of numbers?"

"Of course! One, two, three, four, five, six, seven, eight, nine, ten. Or in French," he said grandly, "it's un, deux, trois—"

"Hah!" she said. "Numbers are just a set of rules that some bonehead made up. They're just the fence he built to keep fools from falling over the edge—"

"What edge?"

"Oh, go and fetch me a bunch of parsley from the garden!"

That was her way of shutting him up when she'd had enough. She liked long spells by herself, did Granny, though she was always pleased to see him again when he came back.

"The arrow → tends to a given value as a limit . . ."

"Timothy!" called his father. "Aunt Di says it's lunchtime."

"Okay! Coming!"

"Did I see you drop a bit of paper down the well just now?"

"Yes, I did," he admitted, rather ashamed.

"Well, don't! Just because we don't drink the water doesn't mean that well can be used as a rubbish dump. After dinner you go and fish it out."

"Sorry, Dad."

During the meal his father and Aunt Di were talking

114

about a local court case: a man who had encouraged, indeed trained, his dog to go next door and harass the neighbors, bite their children, and dig holes in the flower-beds. The court had ordered the dog to be destroyed. Aunt Di, a dog lover, was indignant about this.

"It wasn't the dog's fault! It was the owner. They should have had *him* destroyed—or sent him to prison!"

If I had a dog, thought Timothy, I could train it to go and wake Miss Evans every night by barking under her window, so that she'd fall asleep in class. Or it could get in through her cat-flap and pull her out of bed . . .

"Wake up, boy, you're half asleep," said his father. "It's all that mooning over schoolbooks, if you ask me. You'd better come and help me cart feed this afternoon."

"I've got to finish my math first. There's still loads to do."

"They give them too much homework, if you ask *me*," said Aunt Di. "Addles their minds."

"Well, you get that bit of paper out of the well, anyway," said his father.

He could see it, glimmering white, down below; it had caught on top of the bucket, which still hung there, though nobody used it. He had quite a struggle to wind it up—the handle badly needed oiling, and shrieked at every turn. At last, leaning down, he was able to grab the crumpled sheet; then he let go of the handle, which whirled round crazily as the bucket rattled down again.

But, strangely enough, the crumpled sheet was blank. Timothy felt half relieved, half disappointed; he had been curious to see if his drawing of Old Fillikin was as nasty as he had remembered. Could he have crumpled up the wrong sheet? But no other had any picture on it. At last he decided that the damp atmosphere in the well must have faded the pencil marks. The paper felt cold, soft, and pulpy—rather unpleasant. He carried it indoors and poked it into the kitchen coal-stove.

Then he did another hour's work indoors, scrambling through the problems somehow, anyhow; Miss Evans would be angry again, they were certain to be wrong—but, for heaven's sake, he couldn't spend the whole of Saturday at the horrible task. He checked the results, where it was possible to do so, on his little pocket calculator; blessed, useful little thing, it came up with the results so humbly and willingly, flashing out solutions far faster than his mind could. Farmers need math too, he remembered Miss Evans saying; but when I'm a farmer, he resolved, I shall have a computer to do all those jobs, and I'll just keep to the practical work.

Then he was free, and his father let him drive the tractor, which of course was illegal, but he had been doing it since he was ten and drove better than Kenny the cowman. "You can't keep all the laws," his father said. "Some just have to be broken. All farmers' sons drive tractors. Law's simply a system invented to protect fools—" as Granny had said about the numbers.

That night Timothy dreamed that Old Fillikin came up out of the well and went hopping and flopping away across the fields in the direction of Markhurst Green, where Miss Evans lived. Timothy followed, in his dream, and saw the ungainly yet agile creature clamber in through the cat-flap. *"Don't!* Oh, please, *don't!"* he tried to call. "I didn't mean—I never meant *that*—"

He could hear the flip-flop as it went up the stairs, and he woke himself, screaming, in a tangle of sheet and blanket.

On Sunday night the dream was even worse. That night he took his little calculator to bed with him, and made it work out the nine-times table until there were no more places on the screen.

Then he recited Granny's hymn: "Every morning the red sun Rises warm and bright, But the evening soon comes on And the dark cold night."

If only I could stop my mind working, he thought. He remembered Granny saying, "If we could find Reynard's treasure in Husterloo wood, *I* could stop knitting, and *you* could stop thinking." He remembered her saying, "Kings die standing, that's the way I mean to die."

At last he fell into a light, troubled sleep.

On Mondays, math was the first period, an hour and a half. He had been dreading it, but in another way he was desperately anxious to see Miss Evans, to make sure that she was all right. In his second dream, Old Fillikin had pushed through her bedroom door, which stood ajar, and hopped across the floor. Then there had been a kind of silence filled with little fumbling sounds; then a most blood-curdling scream—like the well handle, as the bucket rattled down.

It was only a dream, Timothy kept telling himself as he rode to school on the bus; nothing but a dream.

But the math class was taken by Mr. Gillespie. Miss

117

Evans, they heard, had not come in. And, later, the school grapevine passed along the news. Miss Evans had suffered a heart attack last night; died before she could be taken to hospital.

When he got off the bus that evening and began to cross the dusk-filled fields towards home, Timothy walked faster than usual, and looked warily about him.

Where—he could not help wondering—was Old Fillikin now?

Aidan Chambers

Dead Trouble

The trouble with being dead is that no one believes you are alive. Things were different years ago. Or so I'm told by others better able to know than myself. In earlier times people still believed in God and the Devil, and therefore, of course, in ghosts. But nowadays all that has changed.

Only last week, for instance, one of the oldest inhabitants in these parts made a chilling appearance at a party where the guests were playing Ouija. But instead of being received with shocked horror, he was laughed at. Imagine it! The guests laughed and said he wasn't there at all, that they had all had too much to drink, which, along with the Ouija, had affected their imaginations, making them *think* they saw a ghost. My own experiences in the last few months, since I was forced to take up this way of life, have been pretty humiliating, but this treatment of an expert, senior ghost, a professional you might say, was a scandal. People here talked about it for days, and the poor fellow himself was so upset he spent every night for weeks afterwards lying around sulking invisibly. And I don't blame him; the whole business was dispiriting.

But I'd better begin at the beginning, otherwise I'll never get to the purpose of this message.

Three months ago I fell into the concrete-mixer at work. The mixer was a huge affair, not one of those little ones you see churning away on small building sites. We made bulk concrete in it, ready for transporting in large quantities by truck to major constructions. At any rate, I fell in. I blame myself really; it was no one else's fault. I should have kept my mind on my work instead of thinking about Veronica. (She was my girlfriend at the time, and was being a bit troublesome.)

Before I go on, I must explain that death is quite different viewed from my present situation than it is viewed from yours. As with most things in life—or after it, come to that—death does not seem half so bad when it is all over as you think it is going to be before it happens. Just like going to the dentist is worse to think about beforehand than it is when you get there, and is often quite a laugh afterwards. Well, dying is just the same; we here are always laughing about it, especially when people have just arrived—it is such a relief to them, and they wonder what all the fuss was about.

Like so many "modern" people, I used to think death meant the end of everything. Blackout. Kaput. The finish. Needless to say, I know differently now. (Mind you, there have been times during the last few months when I have wished my death really had been the end!)

120

Death is like everything else in another way too. Some people die lucky; others don't. I didn't. Though up till my death I had been pretty fortunate, the episode with the concrete-mixer seemed to change all that. I haven't had a stroke of luck since.

Let me explain.

When I slipped into the mixer, I was on my own. My mate Harry was having his tea break; I was keeping things going until he returned to relieve me. But when he got back I had gone. He isn't particularly bright, isn't Harry, and he didn't think of looking in the mixer for me. He thought I'd gone off sick.

At home, my family (father, mother, sister) started worrying when I didn't get in that night. But they waited until the following morning before they informed the police. After a bit of investigating, everyone decided I must have run off, and the police put me on the missing persons list.

Meanwhile, of course, I had been churning round with the half-mixed concrete. I hadn't expected to fall in so I escaped the awful business of knowing I was going to die, though as it turned out, it wasn't such an ordeal as you might suppose. For a start, it was over quickly. A slip of the foot, a nasty couple of minutes swilling about with the sand and gravel and cement and water, and I was dead. (I didn't much care for the gravel—I've always had a fairly sensitive skin—but the change of state from what I was to what I am now happened in the blink of an eye, and was really rather a pleasant sensation. Like sliding into sleep.)

My death having happened, I was in a position to watch

developments without feeling a thing. Or, to put it more accurately, without feeling anything that was being done to my "mortal remains": my corpse.

When Harry got back from his tea break, he transferred the load of mixed concrete into a truck, and as my remains were by then well mixed with the concrete, they were transferred to the truck too. The truck drove off to a building site in central Manchester, and there the load of concrete (and my corpse) was poured straight into a mould for a stanchion that was to be used as one of the main supports of a new office block.

And there my remains remain, cased in concrete, fifty feet above ground, and now quite solid. (As one of my less tasteful companions put it, a rather stiff stiff. I did not reward his unseemly remark with even the ghost of a smile.)

Being sealed in a pillar of concrete, however, is the cause of the trouble I now find myself in. For, unfortunately, no one knows my earthly remains are there. No one, that is, who hasn't yet died. Worse still, no one knows I'm dead. Which is why my spiritual being is trapped here in this ghostly condition. As far as I can gather, one of the reasons, among many, why people get stuck between "life" and "after life" is that their deaths are unknown to their earthbound relatives.

(I was very surprised, I might tell you, to discover how many people get caught in this state of being, for all kinds of reasons. You expect to find murderers, of course, and there are plenty—though on the whole they turn out to be jolly nice blokes; but I was taken aback at the number of schoolteachers, for example, and politicians and army

122

officers. The teachers and politicians spend most of their time trying to talk their way out into the "after life," and never succeed. The army officers, however, take to this life very well. They enjoy going on what they call "chill jaunts"—the kind of haunting that makes earthbound people scream and turn pale. I need hardly add they do this as badly as most of them did everything else in their earth life. Not that this matters much, for with its loss of popularity among earth people, ghostly haunting is rather a disappointing occupation these days. Everybody here is in very low spirits about it.)

But I'm rambling again. It's one of the hazards of being a ghost. You have so much time on your hands and very little to do with it.

As I say, being caught in the in-between, ghostly life— a kind of limbo-land between mortality and eternity—is a bit of a bore, and my aim is to pass on as quickly as possible. But to do this, my relatives must be informed of my death. And as they are not likely to discover my remains in their present secure location, the chances of my parents discovering my death are pretty slim. So I decided I must somehow or other get a message to them.

You have no idea how difficult it is to get a simple message from the "dead" to the "living"! The living just won't listen; and this present climate of disbelief in the afterlife only makes the task more difficult. I asked some of the older ghosts round here for advice. Everyone told me the same thing: don't bother. It would be a waste of time and energy, they said, and I'd only end up getting the jitters. I know now what they meant: talking to people who pretend you aren't there is worse than being sent to

123

coventry. At least when people send you to coventry they don't pretend you aren't there; they just ignore you.

However, being a newcomer to the ghostly life, I refused to listen to such good advice. They were all old codgers, I told myself, spirits whose energies were worn out, sapped by years of failure. They had stopped trying ("given up the ghost" seemed hardly the right expression under the circumstances). What was wanted was a little enterprise, a little originality, and, most of all, some determination. I believed I possessed all three in quantity. My older companions smiled tolerantly, as wise old men always do when confronted with youthful foolishness, and drifted away to enjoy themselves at their leisure.

So, heedless of good counsel, I set to work. Two factors led to my first method of attempting to get in touch. First, though I wanted to communicate with my relatives, I did not want to upset them by suddenly materializing unannounced in the front room at home while they were watching television. They might have joined me in my present state, dispatched here by shock. Dad, after all, had a weak heart, and Mum has always been of a nervous disposition. I did think of contacting my girlfriend Veronica, who, in a way, was responsible for the situation I am now in. But she had already taken up with another fellow, and the one thing that was clear to me even then was that it is useless trying to make contact with mortals who have lost all interest in you, as well as having no belief in ghosts anyway. Veronica had certainly lost interest in me within a couple of days of my "disappearance," as I knew from what I had observed of her evenings out with her new boyfriend (the one who was causing the trouble that started me thinking that led to me slipping into the concrete-mixer!). As for ghosts—Veronica went all through the film of *Nightmare House* without a twinge of fear, while it scared me for weeks. Veronica was out!

The second thing that decided me on my first course of action was that, being a novice at materialization and ghostly activities in general, it was easier to appear at the place of my death than anywhere else. That meant a haunting of the mixing yard at work.

Fine, I thought; just right. I'll do my stuff in front of Harry, and I'll appear looking just as I did on the fatal day, dressed in my overalls. He'll be sure to recognize me then, and be less likely to get the willies, thinking he is seeing any old ghost.

With the confidence that ignorance inspires in men, I went through the materialization routine and successfully took my former shape three feet from Harry at four-thirty on the afternoon of the Thursday following the day I died. It was a beautiful day, the sun shining from a blue sky as it sank towards the spring evening. Harry was tending the mixer stripped down to his vest he was so warm.

I stood there in front of him for a full minute and more, waiting for him to catch sight of me. I nodded and smiled in a friendly way so that he would know I wasn't a malevolent type (we had, after all, had our arguments from time to time). He kept glancing at me, but showed not a flicker of reaction. At first this didn't bother me; he's a slow-witted lad. But then I started to lose patience. I waved at him, danced about a bit, even took a step nearer to him. He would have to be blind not to see me now, I thought.

Then I heard a cough at my elbow. I dematerialized to find an old ghost by the name of Cathcart Fitzgammon standing by my side. He was tut-tutting in a haughty manner, and shaking the grey-haired locks he insists on keeping so as to retain his eighteenth-century looks.

"Dash it, young feller," he said. "You'll do no good like that."

I felt a bit bad-tempered that he had interrupted my very first haunt in such a way.

"Why not?" I snapped.

"Daylight haunts needs considerable skill and experience, old chap," he said. "Besides which, you were standing with the setting sun right behind you. That poor mortal whose attention you hoped to attract would never have seen you, no matter how bright you managed to make your appearance. You haven't a hope in . . . er . . . on Earth of catching his eye. If I were you I'd have a go during the night. It's easier then."

He drifted off without another word, chuckling to himself.

Of course, I had to admit that Cathcart was right. He had also put me off my stroke, and I needed time to collect myself again. So I postponed operations for an hour or two while I considered the situation.

The difficulty was that if I appeared in daylight Harry would probably not see me, but if I waited until dark, or dusk even, Harry would have gone home, so that there would be no one to communicate with anyhow, and I'd be left shivering and alone in the cold.

As far as I could see, there was only one solution. I found Harry's car in the works' car-park, dissolved inside, and made myself comfortable on the back seat, intending to wait until Harry knocked off work and went home. Then, when he went out for the evening, I'd materialize on the passenger seat beside him at a convenient moment and tell him my news. That way I'd know where Harry was when darkness fell, saving myself ohms of energy flying about looking for him.

Car-parks are dismal places, as much for ghosts as mortals—which is why you rarely hear of hauntings in them—and there was no one about of my kind to pass the time of day with; so very soon I was bored, and what with the bright sun and the stuffy warmth of Harry's car, I very soon dozed off. (There's nothing like bright light and warmth for setting a ghost nodding.) Half an hour after dissolving into Harry's car I was as dormant as a flat battery.

I came to hours later. Night had fallen, and was encouragingly black, without stars or moon. It was so black, I thought at first the car must be parked in Harry's garage. But then I heard a noise from the front seat that indicated very clearly that we weren't in Harry's garage at all. I looked up and there was Harry, necking with his girlfriend, a shapely lass from the accounts office at work. We were parked under some trees in a lay-by just out of town.

Naturally, I felt a little uncomfortable. I'm not one of those ghosts who go round peeping at friends they've left behind, enjoying the sight of them in all kinds of situations both public and private. (Personally, I think that's as sick an occupation for a ghost as it is for a mortal.) But I'd spent a good deal of time and energy already keeping up with Harry so that I could get my message to him, and I wasn't going to give in now.

I had to act quickly, before things got really embarrassing. Without another thought I went through the drill for materialization at double-quick pace. Unfortunately, in my haste I put too much energy into some parts of the drill and not enough into others, and was rather careless overall. My lack of experience as a haunter, you see! The result was astonishing, and, but for the circumstances, might have been both interesting and amusing.

The materialization got completely out of control. Instead of appearing as myself in a gentle glow of unearthly light, I came out as a collection of very violent, phosphorescent colors revealing a hideous object with an enormous head, twisted features, a bloated body, and unfinished, stunted arms and legs.

I did not realize at first just how I looked, for, of course, my attention was fully directed at Harry's back so that I should be ready to speak soothing words as soon as he turned round. So, thinking all was well, I coughed politely to attract his attention. But the cough also came out quite unlike what I intended. Instead of a soft, hacking noise, I heard myself produce what I can only describe as a cataract of prolonged and vicious snarls.

At once I knew that something was wrong, took a glance at myself, and immediately felt angry with myself for being so careless. Which only made matters worse. For my annoyance was transmitted into the materialization and imprinted itself on the warped features of the ghostly figure I had projected, turning an already ghastly face into something so horrible that I almost fainted at the sight of it.

The blaze of phosphor colors, the appearance of my misshapen ghost, the imprinting of my anger on its features: all happened in the blinking of an eye. But it was enough to attract Harry's and his girl's attention. They unraveled themselves with incredible speed, swung round in their seats, and came face to face with my apparition just as the snarls that were meant to be a cough broke the silence of the night.

For a split second they stared in wide-eyed disbelief at the appalling creature hovering in the air above the back seat. Stunned shock was replaced by nerve-shattered fear. The blood drained from their faces; their mouths dropped open. Then each one let out an hysterical scream.

This brought me to my senses. I dematerialized with such speed that the warped and shining figure I had created, instead of fading away, exploded like a searchlight bulb fusing from a short-circuit. The car was plunged into a blackness that seemed, by contrast with the brief brilliance of my ghostly glow, to be tangible.

I had no time to think how I might remedy my awful error. Harry's girl flung open the car door and ran in blind terror screaming into the night. Harry was only a heartbeat behind.

They left me exhausted on the back seat.

It took me an hour to collect my thoughts and reorganize my energy, after which I felt so disappointed I trailed off home to my concrete pillar and stayed there for two days, suffering from acute depression.

Ghost friends tell me I should have been more than pleased with myself. They pointed out, in their efforts to cheer me up, that in these days of disbelief in specters I should be proud at my success in scaring two mortals out of their wits. But I'm afraid I couldn't see it like that. I had made a hash of the thing I really wanted to do; and I had been professionally careless. There was no excuse for such things. And as a result I was paying the price: I was still slopping round in ghostly limbo. Not that it is a bad life, as lives go. But it is not the ultimate . . . not the life any sane soul desires. And when you are within range of that life, as I am now that I am dead, the desire becomes a yearning almost painfully strong. The wise old man who said that Hell is the yearning to be in Heaven was right after all. But I cannot satisfy that yearning until I can persuade some mortal that I *am* dead, that my earthly remains are safely stowed away among the steel girders and concrete pillars of the Sure Shield Insurance Building, Manchester.

Two days' rest worked wonders. I got over my depression, recharged myself, did a good deal of thinking. The third day I spent discussing my new ideas with the most experienced ghosts who lived within convenient range of my billet in the pillar. The consensus of opinion was that I had two possible courses of action open to me. Neither was easy to pull off successfully.

I chose spirit possession first.

To get the best results from spirit possession you need an emotionally unstable mortal with a vivid imagination and a mind open to suggestion. All the experts told me that teenage girls are admirable for the purpose. And I knew just the right one for me. My sister.

Angela is sixteen. She is emotionally so unstable that she is as happy as a lark one minute and weeping like a sick willow the next. Her imagination is vivid to the point of being lurid (at any rate, it allows her to see pimply teenage boys as Greek gods, which anyone has to admit takes a powerful imagination). As for her mind, it is as pliant as warm plasticine. On the other hand, like most girls of her age, her constitution is as tough as tempered steel, so I had no fears of any ill effects on her health if my still rather amateur ghosting went badly wrong, as it had done with Harry. (Harry, by the way, recovered his car the next day in broad daylight, after which he had the local vicar exorcize it—something I regarded as extravagant cheek, seeing he never goes near a church from one year's end to the next.)

Angela would do nicely. She also had the added advantage of being one of the family; she would know who and what I was taking about without tiresome and lengthy explanations.

The only trouble was that possession takes a day or two to get going properly. Had I appreciated before I began how much hard work goes into it on the ghost's part, I'd certainly have dropped the entire idea at once. As it was, I went ahead with enthusiasm.

I gave the first night up to dream-making. Well before Angela's normal bedtime I settled myself in her room, and began to compose myself for the task ahead, inventing the dreams I'd put into Angela's head once I'd got inside her—a tricky business in itself. When her bedtime came, I was fully in the spirit of the occasion.

Angela's bedtime came, but Angela did not. She did not even arrive home from an evening out until twelve-thirty. By then my concentration was already a bit frayed; instead of feeling calm, collected, and spiritually prepared, I was irritable, out of joint, and sparking all over the place with nasty thoughts about my sister. I recalled ruefully that this was exactly the effect Angela had usually had on me during our earthly life together.

When at last she arrived home, Dad was waiting to haul her over the coals for being out so late without permission. They argued. Angela flounced up to her room. By this time she was in no condition for me or anyone else to possess in any way at all. After slamming her door, she crashed round her room for a quarter of an hour giving vent to her temper; then for ten minutes she wept soulfully on her bed just loudly enough for the parents to hear her but not so loud that either of them would come in and console her. Finally, she pulled off her clothes, threw them in a heap on the floor, and fell bad-tempered into bed, where she lay awake for ages inventing the most lurid and morbid fantasies I have yet encountered in anyone's mind, fantasies involving Dad, her boyfriend (who had kept her out late), and herself (in dramatic, romantic, and, needless to add, tragic situations).

I could hardly summon up enough brotherly affection and tenderness to go on with my plan. Indeed, for a while I was sorely tempted to give her the most blood-curdling, spine-chilling haunt I could manage, just to teach her a lesson. But eventually she drifted off to sleep and I pulled myself together and went to work.

You'll appreciate that, at this point, I must leave out technical details. The method by which one gets inside another person to control their thoughts is difficult enough to explain to a spirit; it is almost impossible to do so to a mortal. But should a mortal by some chance understand the explanation, then they would possess information that would give them a power over others of an extraordinary kind. If this power fell into the wrong hands you can see what evil could be let loose in the world.

All I can say is that for a couple of hours I gave Angela the treatment. I started out with pleasant memory dreams. I used one about the two of us years ago when she was still very small and I saved her from drowning in a seaside pool all of six inches deep. At least I told Mum I had saved her, and Angela was only too glad to take part in the deception because it sounded such a dramatic story and she was the center of it. I used the one about the Christmas when she was thirteen and I gave her the first pair of nylons she had ever owned, along with a gigantic box of Swiss chocolates (a rather spiteful gift actually, as she was trying to slim at the time, being just at the puppy-fat age). Then I brought back the time when I stood up for her against Mum and Dad; Angela wanted to stay out late at a party for the first time in her life. (This seemed an appropriate memory to recall, considering the events of the night.)

There was lots more of this kind of thing before I decided she had had enough. I juggled everything about, of course, and exaggerated bits here, suppressed unpleasant details there, and generally colored the dreams so that everything was larger than life: a real potpourri of a dream, it was. By the time I was finished Angela was in a very receptive mood indeed, whimpering with nostalgia for the happy times we'd had together. (In fact, we were always bickering and back-biting; but time and dreams, and death most of all are powerful antidotes to people's recollections of the truth, as you'll have noticed, I expect.)

133

This done, I was ready to start on the big scene, a surrealist nightmare that Salvador Dali would have been proud to invent. Angela saw me in every deadly situation imaginable. I fell from a cliff into swirling, angry waves over which the sun shone, but a sun that looked like a huge illuminated clock with the hands showing three-thirty— the time at which I slipped into the mixer. I pictured her stirring a pan of porridge (she hates porridge); she saw an insect threshing about in the pan, looked closer, saw it was not an insect but me! At that moment I disappeared under the surface and the oven clock rang its alarm bell with the hands pointing to three and six. On and on, until Angela was in a sweat of anxiety and was beginning to suspect what I wanted her to: that I was dead, and not just "missing." In the end she was moaning, and shaking her head in her sleep, as if saying "No, no!"

All this took a vast amount of energy, and I was soon dangerously tired. I decided that, before things got out of control, I should get some rest and observe the outcome of my first night's work. But, just to make sure that Angela did not dismiss her dreams when she woke up, I waited until the morning light brought her back to consciousness. Then, as soon as she opened her eyes, I picked up a bottle of cold cream from her dressing-table and hurled it across the room.

That did it. Angela was out of bed and into Mum's room without a second thought. There she poured out her confused dreams, confusing them all the more by trying to recount them to someone else. Mum thought Angela was ill; Dad as always listened calmly and said nothing.

Angela insisted that her dreams were an omen, that I had not gone off somewhere secretly as everyone said, but that I had died somehow, and not very pleasantly. Mum burst into tears and told Angela not to talk like that. "Where there's life there's hope," she said. (I told you people no long believe you're alive when you're dead!) Angela then burst into tears too, said no one ever had understood her but me, that she knew, just *knew*, her dreams meant that I was dead, and that she felt like running away and never coming back. Dad sighed deeply and got up, saying he felt like a nice cup of tea. After this, Angela stormed from the room, dressed hurriedly, and left for school without eating any breakfast or saying another word.

I had the uneasy feeling that my attempt to get a message to my family via Angela was doomed to failure. But I pressed on.

The next night I repeated the dreams, but this time I ended them by engraving a mental picture of myself in a tragic pose deep in Angela's mind before throwing a few things round the room in best poltergeist fashion just as she woke up.

Once again Angela ran to Mum. She was so desperately convincing and distressed that Mum took her seriously, listening sympathetically to her story. Mum even came into Angela's room to see the mess I'd made. Dad went off at the first sign of trouble to make himself a cup of tea.

Angela, placated by Mum's sympathy and excited by the effect of her performance—she loves to be the central figure in a drama—set off for school in high spirits, and there recounted her tale to all and sundry, though only after swearing each person to secrecy and telling them it was all in the strictest confidence.

All that day I sat quietly smiling to myself; here was progress after all. Another night and I could reveal myself and the details of my death and departure.

The third night was much the same as the other two, with the addition of a ghostly and audible voice whispering "*Angela . . . Angela . . .*" before my sister dropped off to sleep, and a bout of sleepwalking before I dispossessed her in the morning. I had every hope of complete success.

My hopes were soon dashed.

Angela woke pale, fatigued, and dizzy. I had overdone things.

Mum took one look at the limp figure in the bed and sent for a doctor. There was, of course, nothing seriously the matter with the girl. True, she was tired and running a temperature. But all she needed was a day's rest.

The situation now got out of control. The doctor was suspicious, though he pretended otherwise to Angela. He prescribed a tranquillizer and told her to stay in bed. But downstairs, he told Mum to "keep an eye on that girl and report any change in her condition." Mum was only too delighted to have an opportunity of mothering her only daughter and watched her every minute of the day and as much as she could manage of the following night.

Dad drank endless cups of tea.

Unimportant though these things may appear, they put me in a swivet. The tranquillizers made my task three times more difficult than before; my experience as a ghost was too limited to cope with the powers of modern medical science. Mum on the watch meant that if I tried a haunt she would be sure to see the effects, which would upset her more than I could bear. As for Dad's endless tea drinking: I recognized this as a sure sign that things were getting on top of him and I had even less desire to upset him than I had to upset Mum. If he started worrying, the strain might affect his dicky heart and for all I knew he'd end up joining me. This was a responsibility I dared not take.

For a day or two I let things ride, hoping Angela's health would improve, when I could start work again. But during the doctor's last visit, Mum had a long private chat with him, telling him all about Angela's dreams, and about the things being thrown round her room. The doctor said that he'd thought as much—he'd known at once that something was up. It was, he said, a common ailment among girls of Angela's age; the best thing would be to take Angela to a psychiatrist.

I dropped my plans like a hot brick there and then and fled back to my pillar in the insurance building. Psychiatrists were the last people I wanted to tangle with—or to tangle with my sister; they can make a haunting so complicated and mess one about so much that it just isn't worth the effort. (It doesn't surprise me one bit that this ghostly limbo-land is teeming with psychiatrists; more of them get stuck here than of any profession. And I've never heard of one of them getting through to the other side. Old Freud mopes around, muttering about sex, and Jung is always arguing with him and seeing archetypal patterns in the least likely places and events. They're a hopeless bunch!)

Well, my defeat at Mum's hands left me one more solution worth trying. Automatic writing. If this failed then I was condemned to a desultory life in this ghostly state for years—maybe centuries—until someone accidentally found my remains in the insurance building. Luckily, modern buildings are made to last no more than a few years, so my prospects of being discovered were brighter than those of ghosts whose bodies are buried in ancient buildings that were built to last for ever.

I consulted the experts once more. Having recovered their cool after the shock of hearing any ghost as inexperienced as myself announce that he was taking up automatic writing—something only the most advanced and knowledgeable haunters ever even contemplate—they gave me a lot of useful tips.

They warned me, for instance, not to employ professional mediums and clairvoyants. Professionals, they said, are usually phoney anyway and have never made contact with anything more than their instinct for making money at the expense of the credulous. And those who are genuine spirit contacts, born with the power to speak the words spirit people put into their minds, are just like all actors: they love to add and take away from the original script. Never satisfied to let the spirit work through them, they can't resist adding a touch of detail there, and missing the main point here; while they have an insatiable taste for melodrama: for dressing up in weird clothes, and rigging outlandish gimmicks, and upstaging any poor spirit who is foolish enough to get involved with them. No, my advisers said, they are an odd lot and best left alone.

"What you must do," they told me, "is find an ordinary person who is clairvoyant and doesn't know it. They are the people most likely to have the special make-up of personality you need to work through, while they won't try to take part themselves in writing your message."

I spent five weeks looking round for suitable mortals, ones with the right qualities for such difficult work as I had in mind: people pure in spirit, innocent in nature, neither naïve nor over-wise. Above all they must possess great faith, faith in life as worth living despite its horrors and troubles, faith in human nature and the durability of that incomparably beautiful but elusive creation, the human soul. Such people, I discovered, are rare indeed.

But I found one in the end, though with a little thought I might have realized where to look and searched here first. I came to this old people's home on the edge of town only this evening. A deaf old man lives here, and has done for the last twenty years since his wife died. He has two sons, both big men in business these days and very busy. Too busy ever to come and see the old man. He has a daughter too, but she has her own family to cope with and manages to visit only on special occasions like Christmas and her father's birthday.

So he passes his days alone, reading and thinking and watching the world go by in the silence of his being. For forty years he worked day in, day out as a joiner. He loved his garden, brought his family up as tenderly as he cared for his tomatoes and sweet peas. From his early twenties the pride and joy of his life was his beloved wife; and she doted on him as much as he on her—though she sometimes pretended otherwise. Now she is gone, he is too old to garden, his children are grown up and scattered. At first, after his wife's death, he grieved bitterly; but he conquered his grief, and every day that passes his faith deepens in the world to come.

This is the man who now writes this message for me. My hope is that, when he wakes and finds these hastily scribbled pages by his bedside, the pencil still clutched in his gnarled old hand, he will do me one further act of kindness, like the many others which have passed unnoticed in his life, and convey my news to my family. Or . . .

Perhaps not . . .

I begin to see that this old saint has something to teach me, who should be beyond teaching . . .

Perhaps, old man, it is best that my sudden end and my curious whereabouts remain unknown. Perhaps I need time to dwell as much as you have done on the nature of life and death. Perhaps when I have done this and plumbed the depths of that knowledge I will be ready to pass from this staging post of death into the life eternal—as ready as you are now to pass from mortality into immortality without a stopping place between.

Quite a thought!

Perhaps after all I am in this limbo-land for a purpose I had not understood. Till now.

I'm grateful to you, old man.

But I will leave this message by your side for your eyes only to see. It can be a sign to you that you have not lived in vain. After reading it, do with it as you please.

Peace . . .

Note: *These papers were by the bedside of Mr. James Henry Gibbons on the morning he was found dead, aged seventy-eight. I suppose they are the ramblings of a dying man's imagination.*

Signed: A. C. Harris, Warden, The Hermitage.

Aidan Chambers

Nancy Tucker's Ghost

Tom Driffield was the fastest coachman on the Great North Road. His reputation was country-wide, his services in constant demand. Tom was a big man, strong, handsome, with a soft-toned voice and a gentleness of manner that even his prime coach horses responded to with pleasure. And so dedicated was Tom to his job that he was well into his thirties before he found time to fall in love and think of marriage. When he did, it was Nancy Tucker, the daughter of a Sheriff Hutton farmer, who caught his eye and took his heart.

Nancy was fifteen years younger than Tom, but this meant nothing to her. There were few men in those parts of Yorkshire who possessed Tom's qualities; she had made a good match and she knew it. For his part, Tom was delighted at his good fortune in landing for himself a beautiful young wife-to-be; and he loved the lass deeply.

The wedding day was arranged for the third Sunday in

May. Spring would dress the village in new green, the blossom would be gay and bright, and everyone would be in high spirits after the grey dullness of the long Yorkshire winter.

On the Sunday when the banns were to be called for the first time, Tom unexpectedly had to drive the mail to London. He had been looking forward to attending church with his Nancy, the pair of them decked out in their Sunday best, and ready to receive the congratulations of relatives and congregation.

"I'll think of you all through the service, Tom," said Nancy, kissing her disappointed fiancé; then she laughed. "But mind you aren't driving the mail on our wedding day!"

"I'll have something better to ride that day than a coach and four!" Tom replied. And they laughed together as lovers do and thought the time would never pass between now and the third Sunday in May.

So Tom went off to drive the mail to London, and Nancy, escorted by her father and mother and brothers and sisters, walked to church to hear the banns called.

A moment or two before the service was due to start a young stranger entered the church. Every head turned to look. It was not so much that he was a stranger that attracted people's attention, though that was cause enough, for their village was a quiet place not much visited by anyone. Rather it was the young man's good looks and dashing figure that held their gaze. He had long, jet-black hair, tied at the back of his head by crimson ribbon in a neat little pigtail; his clothes were elegant, colorful, cut to fit closely his well-built body and show off his manly shape; his frills were of the best lace; and as he strode down the aisle to take his seat in one of the front pews, a diamond ring on the first finger of his right hand sparkled in the morning light that streamed through the east window.

The sexton—like everyone else—took the young man for nobility, and allowed him to sit in the private pews. There the stranger made a brief devotion, sat back, and stared unblinking about him, confidently inspecting the congregation.

Nancy, who had never seen such a breathtaking young man, stared at him, noting every detail of his handsome features and expensive, fashionable clothes; and even when the gentleman's eyes fell on hers as he looked about, she could not glance away.

The spell was broken by Mrs. Tucker, who squeezed her daughter's arm to distract her.

"Who is he?" Nancy whispered.

"No doubt a city gent," replied Mrs. Tucker as the congregation stood for the entrance of the choir and vicar.

Though Nancy tried very hard to keep her mind on Tom and the service, her attention wandered often in the next half-hour in the direction of the young stranger across the aisle. And each time her glance strayed that way, her admiring eyes met his steady gaze.

Then came the calling of the banns. Nancy's and Tom's were the only names to be read out. Nancy blushed, and bent her head shyly to avoid the smiling faces that now were turned towards her. During that moment she thought of Tom, and somehow felt uneasy.

Afterwards, outside the church, Nancy stood with her

family while everyone from the vicar to the smallest choir-boy offered congratulations, and joked, teasing her in the way people do newly betrothed couples.

When all were done, the young man, who had been watching from a polite distance, came up to Nancy.

"I take it you are the young lady whose banns I have just heard being called for the first time?" he said, bowing.

"I am, sir," said Nancy, bobbing a curtsy in return.

"May I," went on the stranger, "offer you my heartfelt good wishes."

Before Nancy could reply, he took her hand, raised it to his lips, and kissed it.

"You are kind, sir," said Mrs. Tucker in a sharp, cold tone.

"My mother, sir," said Nancy, hardly knowing where to put herself after the stranger's unexpected behavior.

"Ma'am," said the young man, bowing again more deeply than before. "If I may say so, he is a fortunate fellow who has won the hand of one of the prettiest girls I have ever seen."

Mrs. Tucker inclined her head in acceptance of the stranger's flattery, but said nothing.

Smiling again at Nancy, the gentleman then took his leave and went off towards the village.

"Did you see his great diamond ring!" exclaimed one of Nancy's sisters when the man was out of earshot.

"Did you see his good looks!" said another almost unable to contain herself.

"I saw his fine airs," said Mrs. Tucker with a sniff. "And they did not impress me. It takes more than diamonds and good looks to make a gentleman."

Nancy said nothing; but her eyes followed every step the young man took until he was out of sight.

Three days later Nancy Tucker eloped with the handsome stranger. Her mother learned the news from a letter Nancy left behind, along with a note for Tom in which she explained that she had fallen headlong in love with the young man and hoped Tom would forgive her for her faithlessness.

Sheriff Hutton had not known such a scandal for years. Everyone talked about Nancy's behavior, and soon the story was pieced together.

The young stranger had arrived on the Saturday evening and put up at the village inn. The next day, he had gone to church. That evening he took aside a maid at the inn, pressed a golden guinea into her hand, and asked her to do him a service, secretly. The maid had never had so much money in her life; and when she learned that the stranger wished her to deliver a note to Nancy Tucker, she readily agreed to do as he asked, excited by the prospect of being involved in such a romantic plot. If only, she thought, some dashing young man would send her secret notes! Only when it was discovered that Nancy had eloped did the maid understand the stranger's real purpose. Stricken with guilty grief, she revealed all she knew. She had thought the note would lead to nothing more than a brief and secret tryst between Nancy and the stranger; now she knew she had been bribed into taking part in something far more serious.

Tom, of course, was hurt more than anyone by the

sudden and unexpected turn of events. Inwardly, he grieved and suffered the pain of wounded love; but being the man he was, never a word of bitterness did he speak against Nancy. It was towards himself that he directed the blame for what had happened. Had he given up his turn on the mail coach that fatal Sunday he would have been in church by Nancy's side, and able to protect her from the advances of the handsome stranger—who, it seemed, was no gentleman at all, for he had left the village without paying his bill at the inn.

Nor was Tom a man to be broken by such misfortune. He threw himself with even more energy into his work to keep his mind from brooding on his loss. The following winter he married a woman from Thirsk and settled in the town with his new bride.

This might well have been the end of the matter. But in March of the next year Tom was driving his coach towards London a few miles north of York when he saw a woman with a small baby clutched in her arms standing by the roadside. The woman was a ragged and pathetic sight, and plainly in need of help. Tom stopped the coach and climbed down. Only then did he recognize the sick woman. It was Nancy.

"Dear God," Tom exclaimed, distressed beyond words by the changed and ailing figure before him. "Nancy! Poor lass! Into the coach with you. I'll get ye to a doctor."

Too weak to move or speak, Nancy gazed at Tom as though he were an angel out of Heaven.

Gently, Tim lifted her into the coach and wrapped her in a traveling blanket. Then he whipped up the horses and drove as fast as he dared into York. There he put Nancy into a room in an inn and ran out for a doctor while the innkeeper's wife tended her.

The doctor's report was dismal. Taking Tom aside after examining Nancy and the baby, he told him that neither Nancy nor the child had long to live—no more perhaps than a few hours.

All that night Tom sat by Nancy's bed. From time to time she would wake from her fitful sleep; each time her eyes would find Tom's and gaze lovingly at him. Then came a moment, in the middle of the night, when, waking from her sleep, the dying woman managed to speak.

"Dear Tom," she said, her voice no more than a dry whisper. "Have you no word of reproach for me?"

Moved almost to tears, Tom could only shake his head.

Pausing now and again to catch her breath, Nancy went on to relate all that had happened in the months since last they were together. The dashing young man had carried Nancy off to Northallerton, where they had been married. Only then did she discover her husband was far from being the rich and noble gentleman she had taken him for. He was, in fact, a highwayman. Worse, as the days went by he revealed his true nature: vicious, cruel, mean.

They had not been long together when Nancy discovered she was pregnant. When her husband learned of this, he laughed, told her he was not her husband at all; he was married already to a woman in the south. He had gone through the wedding ceremony only to please Nancy and so possess her. It was all, he thought, a huge joke, a delicious adventure.

But not to Nancy. At once, she left, and managed to

find a job as a servant-girl in a big house. But it was not long before her master realized Nancy was pregnant. He flew into a fit of moral rage, and threw her out of the house and warned all his friends for miles about against her. Unable to get a job, moneyless, and too ashamed to go back home, Nancy wandered the moors tortured by regrets and finding what food and shelter she could. On those bare and windswept hills she gave birth to her child, and, as soon as she could move, staggered to the roadside where Tom had found her those few hours ago.

Never a man to whom words came easily, Tom listened to the story in silence. But inside him he felt burning anger against the man who had brought such suffering to his beloved Nancy; while for Nancy herself his heart bled with pity.

When the story was finished, he hung his head in his hands and groaned.

"Nancy . . . oh, Nancy . . ."

"Do not grieve, dear Tom," Nancy whispered. "It is over now. And I have the happiness of dying with your face to look upon and your love to comfort me."

"Don't speak of death!" Tom murmured, but his voice carried no conviction, for he could see she had little longer to live.

Nancy smiled.

"You have been kinder to me than I deserve, Tom," she said: "And I shall repay your kindness. If ever you or yours are in need, I shall come back to help you . . . see if I don't . . ."

She spoke no more. Her eyes closed. And this time she fell into a deeper sleep than she had ever known before.

The poor, newborn baby at her side followed its mother out of this world only moments later.

Only then did Tom Driffield let his tears flow.

Two years went by. One day Tom was commissioned to drive four important passengers from Durham to York. When he arrived to collect them, the passengers were eager to be off.

"Get us to York by eight o'clock this evening," said one as they climbed into the coach, "and I'll treble your charge for the journey."

Tom looked at the time and calculated how long he usually took to make the trip from Durham to York. To cover the distance by eight o'clock that day was asking almost more than was possible. But with luck, good weather, and no accidents, he might just earn his prize. He set off at a spanking pace, determined to meet the challenge.

All went well until, only seven miles outside York, fog came down so thick that Tom could hardly see Marquis, the leading horse of his four. It was madness to go on in such conditions.

He reined the horses in, stopped the coach, and climbed down.

"Unless this fog lifts in the next few minutes, gentlemen, we haven't a hope of reaching York by eight, even if we make it at all tonight."

"But surely you are going on, man?" said one of the party.

"I'd usually wait until such treacherous fog as this has lifted, sir," Tom said. " 'Twould be foolhardy to go on."

"Try, coachman," said one of the passengers. "We *must* do all we can to be in York by eight."

"I'm sorry, sir, but . . ."

"I'll double your payment yet again if you get us there."

"It isn't money I'm after," Tom replied sharply.

"We implore you, coachman," said another of the passengers. "It really is a matter of great importance to us."

"Well, if it means so much to you, gentlemen, I'll do my best. But I cannot take responsibility for any ill consequences."

"We realize that. Go on, go on."

Tom climbed back on to his box. As he did so, he saw with surprise a figure sitting in his seat, holding the reins. The figure turned its head and looked at him.

"Nancy!" he cried in astonishment.

And Nancy it was—or rather her ghost!

"You've kept your promise, I see," Tom said, smiling.

The specter said nothing, but smiled back at him, shook the reins, and set the horses off at a gallop.

Tom and his four passengers had good cause to remember every inch of the next seven miles of their journey. The fog swirled round them; the coach, driven at full pelt, hurled itself over the pitted and stony road with reckless force; the horses strained and sweated and careered onwards as though driven by Jehu himself. Inside the lurching coach the battered passengers hung on for dear life, speechless with fear. But Tom, watching Nancy's ghost, as grey and intangible as the fog itself, felt not a twinge of terror. Indeed, he was enjoying himself as much as a child on a fairground carousel.

151

York, when they reached it, was shrouded in fog more thick than ever. But there was no slackening of the mad progress of the speeding coach and four. Nancy guided them through the twisty streets, skidding round narrow corners, and leaving a trail of amazed townspeople diving for safety behind them.

Five minutes before the city clocks chimed eight o'clock, Nancy pulled the horses to a stop outside the Black Swan Inn, their steaming bodies and panted breaths giving off such clouds into the air that the horses themselves seemed to be the makers of the fog.

Without a second's pause, the ghost turned to Tom with a smile, put the reins in his hands, and vanished from sight.

Tom laughed to himself.

"Thanks, Nancy," he muttered to the vacant air. Then louder, he called to his passengers, "Five to eight, gentlemen. You have a minute or two to collect your wits!"

The four men stumbled out of the coach, shaken and incredulous.

"By God," said one, "I'll swear no other man in England has ever been driven like that!"

"No man in England has had such a driver!" Tom replied.

"Your money, coachman," said the leader of the party handing Tom a pouch of silver coins. "And thank you from us all."

"Thank Nancy, not me," said Tom.

"What's that you say?" called the passenger.

" 'Tis nothing, sir, nothing," replied Tom, and drove off his horses to the stables.

So it was that Nancy Tucker kept her word. Many times afterwards she came to Tom Driffield's aid, always when he most needed help that no human, living soul could give him. In time Nancy's ghost became a legend in the north of England, but after Tom's death she appeared no more. She had paid her debt to the man she loved.

Edward Bulwer-Lytton

The Haunted and the Haunters

or

The House and the Brain

Edited and abridged by Aidan Chambers

A friend of mine, who is a man of letters and a philosopher, said to me one day, as if between jest and earnest, "Fancy! Since we last met, I have discovered a haunted house in the midst of London."

"Really haunted? And by what? Ghosts?"

"Well, I can't answer that question; all I know is this: six weeks ago my wife and I were in search of a furnished apartment. Passing a quiet street, we saw on the window of one of the houses a sign, 'Apartments Furnished.' The situation suited us; we entered the house, liked the rooms, engaged them by the week—and left them the third day.

No power on earth could have reconciled my wife to stay longer; and I don't wonder at it."

"What did you see?"

"It was not so much what we saw or heard that drove us away, as it was terror which seized both of us whenever we passed by the door of a certain unfurnished room, in which we neither saw nor heard anything. Accordingly, on the fourth morning I told the woman who kept the house that the rooms did not quite suit us, and we would not stay out our week. She said, dryly, 'I know why: you have stayed longer than any other lodger. Few ever stayed a second night; none before you a third. But I take it they have been very kind to you.'

" 'They? Who?' I asked, affecting to smile.

" 'Why, they who haunt the house, whoever they are. I don't mind them; I remember them many years ago, when I lived in this house, not as a servant; but I know they will be the death of me some day. I don't care; I'm old, and must die soon anyhow. And then I shall be with them, and in this house still.' "

"You excite my curiosity," I said. "Nothing I should like better than to sleep in a haunted house. Pray give me the address of the one you left so ignominiously."

My friend gave me the address; and when we parted, I walked straight to the house. I found it shut up—no sign at the window, and no response to my knock. As I was turning away, a messenger boy said to me, "Do you want anyone at that house, sir?"

"Yes, I heard it was to be let."

"Let! Why, the woman who kept it is dead—has been

dead these three weeks, and no one can be found to stay there, though Mr. Jones, the owner, offered ever so much. He offered Mother, who chars for him, £1 a week just to open and shut the windows, and she would not."

"Would not! And why?"

"The house is haunted: and the old woman who kept it was found dead in her bed, with her eyes wide open. They say the devil strangled her."

"Where does the owner of the house live?"

"In Germyn Street, No. 11."

"What is he—in any business?"

"No, sir, nothing particular; a single gentleman."

I was lucky enough to find Mr. Jones at home. I told him my name and business. I said I heard the house was considered to be haunted; that I had a strong desire to examine it, and that I would be greatly obliged if he would allow me to hire it, though only for a night. I was willing to pay whatever he asked for that privilege.

"Sir," he said with great courtesy, "the house is at your service, for as short or as long a time as you please. Rent is out of the question. I cannot let it, for I cannot even get a servant to keep it in order or answer the door. Unluckily, the house is haunted, if I may use that expression, not only by night, but by day; though at night the disturbances are of a more unpleasant and sometimes of a more alarming character. The poor old woman who died in it three weeks ago was, in her childhood, known to some of my family and was the only person I could ever induce to remain in the house."

"How long is it since the house acquired this sinister character?" I asked.

"That I can scarcely tell you, but very many years since. The old woman I spoke of said it was haunted when she rented it between thirty and forty years ago. The fact is that my life has been spent in the East Indies, and I returned to England only last year."

"Have you never had a curiosity yourself to pass a night in that house?"

"Yes. I passed not a night, but three hours in broad daylight alone in that house. My curiosity is not satisfied, but it is quenched. I have no desire to renew the experiment. I honestly advise you not to spend a night in that house."

"My interest is exceedingly keen," said I, "and my nerves have been seasoned in such variety of danger that I have the right to rely on them—even in a haunted house."

He said very little more He took the keys of the house out of his bureau and gave them to me. Thanking him for his frankness, I carried off my prize.

Impatient for the experiment, as soon as I reached home I summoned my servant, a young man of gay spirits, fearless temper, and as free from superstitious prejudices as anyone I could think of.

"Francis," said I, "I have heard of a house in London which is decidedly haunted. I mean to sleep there tonight. From what I hear, there is no doubt that something will allow itself to be seen or heard—something, perhaps, excessively horrible. Do you think if I take you with me, I may rely on your presence of mind, whatever may happen?"

"You may trust me, sir!" answered Francis, grinning with delight.

"Very well. Here are the keys of the house; this is the address. Go there now, and select for me any bedroom you please. Since the house has not been inhabited for weeks, make up a good fire, air the bed well, and see, of course, that there are candles as well as fuel. Take with you my revolver and my dagger—so much for my weapons—and arm yourself equally well. If we are not a match for a dozen ghosts, we shall be a sorry couple of Englishmen."

I was engaged for the rest of the day on business. I dined alone, and about half-past nine I put a book into my pocket, and strolled leisurely towards the haunted house. I took with me a favorite dog—an exceedingly sharp, bold, and vigilant bull-terrier; a dog fond of prowling about strange ghostly corners and passages at night in search of rats; a dog of dogs for a ghost.

It was a summer night, but chilly, the sky gloomy and overcast. Still, there was a moon—faint and sickly, but still a moon—and if the clouds permitted, after midnight it would be brighter.

I reached the house, knocked, and my servant opened with a cheerful smile.

"All right, sir, and very comfortable."

"Oh!" said I, rather disappointed; "have you not seen nor heard anything remarkable?"

"Well, sir, I must own I have heard something queer."

"What—what?"

"The sound of feet pattering behind me; and once or twice small noises like whispers close at my ear. Nothing more."

"You are not at all frightened?"

"I! Not a bit of it, sir," and his bold look reassured me that, happen what might, he would not desert me.

We were in the hall, the street door closed, and my attention was now drawn to my dog. He had at first run in eagerly enough, but had sneaked back to the door, and was scratching and whining to get out. After being patted on the head and gently encouraged, the dog seemed to reconcile himself to the situation and followed Francis and me through the house, but keeping close at my heels instead of hurrying inquisitively in advance, which was his normal habit in all strange places.

We first visited the kitchen and the cellars, in which there were two or three bottles of wine still left in a bin, covered with cobwebs and evidently undisturbed for many years. For the rest, we discovered nothing of interest. There was a gloomy little backyard with very high walls. The stones of this yard were very damp; and what with the damp and the dust and smoke-grime on the pavement, our feet left a slight impression where we walked.

And now appeared the first strange phenomenon witnessed by myself in this strange house. I saw, just before me, the print of a foot suddenly form itself. I stopped, caught hold of my servant, and pointed to it. In advance of that footprint as suddenly dropped another. We both saw it. I went quickly to the place; the footprint kept advancing before me, a small footprint—the foot of a child. The impression was too faint to distinguish the shape, but it seemed to us both that it was the print of a naked foot. This phenomenon ceased when we arrived at the opposite wall, and it did not repeat itself as we returned.

We remounted the stairs, and entered the rooms on the

159

ground floor, a dining parlor, a small back parlor, and a still smaller third room—all as still as death. We then visited the drawing-rooms, which seemed fresh and new. In the front room I seated myself in an armchair. Francis placed on the table the candlestick with which he had lighted us. I told him to shut the door. As he turned to do so, a chair opposite me moved from the wall quickly and noiselessly and dropped itself about a yard from my own chair, immediately in front of it.

My dog put back his head and howled.

Francis, coming back, had not observed the movement of the chair. He employed himself now in calming the dog. I continued to gaze at the chair, and fancied I saw on it a pale blue misty outline of a human figure, but an outline so indistinct that I could only distrust my own vision. The dog was now quiet.

"Put back that chair opposite me," I said to Francis. "Put it back to the wall."

Francis obeyed. "Was that you, sir?" said he, turning abruptly.

"I! What?"

"Why, something struck me. I felt it sharply on the shoulder—just here."

"No," said I. "But we have jugglers present, and though we may not discover their tricks, we shall catch *them* before they frighten *us*."

We did not stay long in the drawing-rooms; in fact, they felt so damp and so chilly that I was glad to get to the fire upstairs. We locked the doors of the drawing-rooms—a precaution which we had taken with all the rooms we had searched below. The bedroom my servant had selected for me was the best on the floor: a large one, with two windows fronting the street. The four-posted bed, which took up much space, was opposite the fire, which burnt clear and bright. A door in the wall to the left, between the bed and the window, adjoined the room which my servant took for himself. This was a small room with a sofa-bed, and had no other door but the one leading into my bedroom. On either side of my fireplace was a cupboard, without locks, flush with the wall and covered with dull-brown paper. We examined these cupboards—only hooks to suspend dresses; nothing else. We sounded the walls—evidently solid: the outer walls of the building.

Having finished the survey of these rooms, I warmed myself a few moments and lighted my cigar. Then, still accompanied by Francis, went forth to complete my reconnoitre. In the landing-place there was another door; it was closed firmly.

"Sir," said my servant in surprise, "I unlocked this door with all the others when I first came; it cannot have got locked from the inside, for . . ."

Before he had finished his sentence, the door, which neither of us then was touching, opened quietly of itself. We looked at each other. The same thought seized both of us: some human agency might be detected here. I rushed in first, my servant following. A small blank dreary room without furniture . . . a few empty boxes and hampers in a corner . . . a small window, the shutters closed . . . not even a fireplace . . . no other door than that by which we had entered . . . no carpet on the floor, and the floor seemed very old, uneven, worm-eaten, mended here and there. But no living being, and no visible place in which a living being could have hidden. As we stood gazing round, the door by which we had entered closed as quietly as it had opened. We were imprisoned.

For the first time I felt a creep of undefinable horror. Not so my servant. "Why, they don't think to trap us, sir? I could break the door with a kick of my foot."

"Try first if it will open to your hand," said I, "while I unclose the shutters and see what is outside."

I unbarred the shutters; the window looked out on the little backyard I have described. There was no ledge— nothing to break the sheer descent of the wall. No man getting out of that window would have found any footing till he had fallen on the stones below.

Francis, meanwhile, was vainly attempting to open the door. He now turned round to me and asked my permission to use force. I willingly gave him the permission he required. But though he was a remarkably strong man, the door did not even shake to his stoutest kick. Breathless and panting, he stopped. I then tried the door myself, equally in vain. As I ceased from the effort, again that creep of horror came over me; but this time it was more cold and stubborn. I felt as if some strange and ghastly vapor were rising up from the chinks of that rugged floor.

The door now very slowly and quietly opened of its own accord. We rushed out on to the landing. We both saw a large pale light—as large as the human figure but shapeless and unsubstantial—move before us, and climb the stairs that led from the landing into the attics. I followed the light, and my servant followed me. It entered a small garret, of which the door stood open. I entered in the same instant. The light then collapsed into a small globe, exceedingly brilliant and vivid; rested a moment on a bed in the corner, quivered, and vanished.

We approached the bed and examined it—a small one such as is commonly found in attics used by servants. On the chest of drawers that stood near it we saw an old faded silk scarf with the needle still left in a half-repaired tear. The scarf was covered with dust; probably it had belonged to the old woman who had last died in that house, and this might have been her bedroom. I had sufficient curiosity to open the drawers: there were a few odds and ends of female dress, and two letters tied round with a narrow ribbon of faded yellow. I took the letters.

We found nothing else in the room worth noticing, nor did the light reappear. But we distinctly heard, as we turned to go, a pattering footfall on the floor—just ahead of us. We went through the other attics (four, in all), the footfall still preceding us. Nothing to be seen—nothing but the footfall heard. I had the letters in my hand: just as I was descending the stairs I distinctly felt my wrist seized, and a faint, soft effort made to draw the letters from my clasp. I only held them the more tightly, and the effort ceased.

We returned to my room, and I then noticed that my dog had not followed us when we had left it. He was keeping close to the fire, and trembling. I was impatient to examine the letters; and while I read them, my servant opened a little box in which he had the weapons I had ordered him to bring. He took them out, placed them on a table close to my bed-head, and then occupied himself in soothing the dog, who, however, seemed to heed him very little.

The letters were short. They were dated, the dates exactly thirty-five years ago. They were evidently from a lover to his mistress, or a husband to some young wife. A reference to a voyage indicated the writer to have been a seafarer. The spelling and handwriting were those of a man poorly educated, but still the language itself was forceful. In the expressions of endearment there was a kind of rough wild love; but here and there were dark hints at some secret not of love—some secret that seemed of crime. "We ought to love each other," was one of the sentences I remember, "for how everyone else would curse us if all was known." Again: "Don't let anyone be in the same room with you at night—you talk in your sleep." And again: "What's done can't be undone; and I tell you there's nothing against us unless the dead could come to life." Here there was underlined in a better handwriting (a woman's), "They do!" At the end of the letter latest in date the same female hand had written these words: "Lost at sea the 4th of June, the same day as ——."

I put down the letters, and began to think over their contents.

Fearing, however, that the train of thought might unsteady my nerves, I determined to keep my mind in a fit state to cope with whatever the night might bring. I roused myself, laid the letters on the table, stirred up the fire, which was still bright and cheering, and opened my book. I read quietly enough till about half-past eleven. I then threw myself, dressed, upon the bed and told my servant he might retire to his own room, but must keep himself awake. I bade him leave open the door between the two rooms.

164

Thus alone, I kept two candles burning on the table by my bed-head. I placed my watch beside the weapons, and calmly resumed reading. Opposite me the fire burned clear; and on the hearthrug, seemingly asleep, lay the dog. In about twenty minutes I felt an exceedingly cold air pass by my cheek, like a sudden draught. I fancied the door to my right, leading to the landing-place, must have got open. But no—it was closed. I then glanced to my left, and saw the flame of the candles violently swayed as by a wind. At the same moment the watch beside the revolver softly slid from the table—softly, softly—no visible hand—it was gone.

I sprang up, seizing the revolver with one hand, the dagger with the other. I was not willing that my weapons should share the fate of the watch. Thus armed, I looked round the floor. No sign of the watch. Three slow, loud, distinct knocks were now heard at the bed-head.

My servant called out, "Is that you, sir?"

"No. Be on your guard."

The dog now roused himself and sat on his haunches, his ears moving quickly backwards and forwards. He kept his eyes fixed on me with a strange look. Slowly he rose up, all his hair bristling, and stood perfectly rigid, and with the same wild stare. I had no time, however, to examine the dog. Presently, my servant came from his room, and if ever I saw horror in the human face, it was then. I would not have recognized him had we met in the street, so altered was every line.

He passed by me quickly, saying in a whisper that seemed scarcely to come from his lips, "Run—run! It is after me!"

He gained the door to the landing, pulled it open, and

rushed out. I followed him into the landing, calling him to stop; but without heeding me, he bounded down the stairs, clinging to the bannisters, and taking several steps at a time. I heard the street door open—heard it again clap to. I was left alone in the haunted house.

For a brief moment I remained undecided whether or not to follow my servant. But pride and curiosity forbade a flight. I re-entered my room, closing the door after me, and went cautiously into my servant's room. I found nothing to justify his terror. I again carefully examined the walls to see if there were any concealed door. I could find no trace of one—not even a seam in the dull brown paper with which the room was hung. How, then, had the Thing, whatever it was, which had so scared him got in except through my own chamber?

I returned to my room, shut and locked the door between the rooms, and stood on the hearth, expectant and prepared. I now saw that the dog had slunk into an angle of the wall and was pressing himself close against it, as if literally striving to force his way into it. I approached the animal and spoke to it; the poor brute was beside itself with terror. It showed all its teeth, the slaver dropping from its jaws, and would certainly have bitten me if I had touched it. It did not seem to recognize me.

Finding all efforts to soothe the animal in vain, and fearing that his bite might be as poisonous in that state as in the madness of rabies, I left it alone, placed my weapons on the table beside the fire, seated myself, and took up my book.

I soon became aware that something came between the page and the light—the page was overshadowed. I looked up, and I saw what I shall find it very difficult, perhaps impossible, to describe.

It was a Darkness shaping itself from the air in very undefined outline. I cannot say it was of a human form, and yet it was more like a human form, or rather shadow, than anything else. As it stood, wholly apart and distinct from the air and the light around it, its size seemed gigantic, the top nearly touching the ceiling.

While I gazed, a feeling of intense cold seized me. An iceberg before me could not have chilled me more. I feel convinced that it was not the cold caused by fear. As I continued to gaze, I thought—but this I cannot say exactly—that I distinguished two eyes looking down on me from the height. One moment I fancied that I saw them clearly, the next they seemed gone. But still two rays of a pale blue light frequently shot through the darkness, as from the height on which I half believed, half doubted, that I had seen the eyes.

I strove to speak—my voice utterly failed me. I could only think to myself, "Is this fear? It is *not* fear!" I strove to rise—in vain; I felt as if I were weighed down by an irresistible force—that sense of utter inadequacy to cope with a force beyond man's, which one may feel in a storm at sea.

And now, as this impression grew on me, now came, at last, horror—horror to a degree that no words can convey. Still I retained pride, if not courage; and in my own mind I said, "This is horror, but it is not fear; unless I fear I cannot be harmed; my reason rejects this thing. It is an illusion. I do not fear."

With a violent effort I succeeded at last in stretching

out my hand towards the weapon on the table. As I did so, on the arm and shoulder I received a strange shock, and my arm fell to my side powerless. And now, to add to my horror, the light began slowly to wane from the candles; they were not, as it were, extinguished, but their flame seemed very gradually withdrawn; it was the same with the fire—the light went from the fuel; in a few minutes the room was in utter darkness.

The dread that came over me, to be thus in the dark with that dark Thing, brought a reaction of nerve. I found voice, though the voice was a shriek. I remember that I broke forth with words like these: "I do not fear, my soul does not fear." And at the same time I found the strength to rise. Still in that profound gloom I rushed to one of the windows, tore aside the curtain, flung open the shutters. My first thought was—LIGHT. And when I saw the moon high, clear, and calm, I felt a joy that almost drowned the previous terror. There was the moon, there was also the light from the gas-lamps in the deserted street. I turned to look back into the room; the moon penetrated its shadow very palely—but still there was light. The dark Thing, whatever it might be, was gone—except that I could yet see a dim shadow, which seemed the shadow of that Thing, against the opposite wall.

My eye now rested on the table, and from under it there rose a hand, visible as far as the wrist. It was the hand of an aged person—lean, wrinkled, small—a woman's hand. That hand very softly closed on the two letters lying on the table: hand and letters both vanished. There then came the same three loud measured knocks I heard at the bed-head before.

As those sounds slowly ceased, I felt the whole room vibrate; and at the far end there rose, as from the floor, sparks or globes like bubbles of light, many-colored— green, yellow, fire red, azure. Up and down, to and fro, hither, thither, as tiny will-o'-the-wisps the sparks moved slow or swift, each at his own desire. A chair was now moved from the wall without apparent aid, and placed at the opposite side of the table.

Suddenly, from the chair, there grew a shape—a woman's shape. It was distinct as a shape of life, ghastly as a shape of death. The face was young, with a strange mournful beauty: the throat and shoulders were bare, the rest of the form in a loose robe of cloudy white. It began sleeking its long yellow hair, which fell over its shoulders; its eyes were not turned towards me, but to the door; it seemed listening, watching, waiting. The shadow of the Thing in the background grew darker; and again I thought I beheld the eyes gleaming out from the top of the shadow— eyes fixed upon that shape.

As if from the door, though it did not open, there grew out another shape, equally distinct, equally ghastly—a man's shape, a young man's. It was in the dress of the last century. Just as the male shape approached the female, the dark shadow started from the wall, all three for a moment wrapped in darkness. When the pale light returned, the two phantoms were in the grasp of the Thing that towered between them. And there was a bloodstain on the breast of the female. And the phantom male was leaning on its phantom sword, and blood seemed trickling fast from the ruffles, from the lace. And the darkness of the Shadow between swallowed them up. They were gone.

169

And again the bubbles of light shot, and sailed, growing thicker and thicker and more wildly confused in their movements.

The cupboard door to the right of the fireplace now opened, and from it there came the form of an aged woman. In her hand she held letters, the very letters over which I had seen *the* Hand close; and behind her I heard a footstep. She turned round as if to listen, and then she opened the letters and seemed to read. And over her shoulder I saw a livid face, the face of a man long drowned—bloated, bleached, seaweed tangles in its dripping hair. And at her feet lay the form of a corpse, and beside the corpse there cowered a child, a miserable squalid child with famine in its cheeks and fear in its eyes. As I looked in the old woman's face, the wrinkles and lines vanished, and it became a face of youth—hard-eyes, stony, but still youth; and the Shadow darted forth, and darkened over these phantoms as it had darkened over the last.

Nothing now was left but the Shadow, and on that my eyes were intently fixed, till again eyes grew out of the Shadow—evil, serpent eyes. And the bubbles of light again rose and fell and mingled with the wan moonlight. And now from these globes themselves, as from the shell of an egg, monstrous things burst out. The air grew filled with them: larvae so bloodless and so hideous that I can in no way describe them except to remind the reader of the swarming life which the microscope brings before his eyes in a drop of water. Things transparent, supple, agile, chasing each other, devouring each other. Forms like nothing ever seen by the naked eye.

The shapes came round me and round, thicker and faster

170

and swifter, swarming over my head, crawling over my right arm, which was outstretched against the evil beings. Sometimes I felt myself touched, but not by them. Invisible hands touched me. Once I felt the clutch of cold soft fingers at my throat. I was still aware that if I gave way to fear I should be in bodily peril; and I concentrated all my faculties in the single focus of resisting, stubborn will. And I turned my sight from the Shadow—above all from those strange serpent eyes—eyes that had now become distinctly visible. For there, though in nothing else round me, I was aware that there was a WILL, a will of intense evil, which might crush down my own.

The pale atmosphere in the room now began to redden. The larvae grew lurid as things that live in fire. Again the room vibrated; again were heard the three measured knocks; and again all things were swallowed up in the darkness of the dark Thing, as if out of that darkness all had come, into that darkness all returned.

As the gloom retreated, the Shadow was wholly gone. Slowly as it had been withdrawn, the flame grew again into the candles on the table, again into the fuel in the grate. The whole room came once more into sight.

The two doors were still closed, the door leading to the servant's room still locked. In the corner into which he had pushed himself lay the dog. I called to him—no movement. I approached. The animal was dead. His eyes protruded, his tongue out of his mouth, the froth gathered round his jaws. I took him in my arms and brought him to the fire. I felt acute grief for the loss of my poor favorite. I imagined he had died of fright. But I found that his neck was actually broken. Had this been done in the dark? Must

171

it not have been by a hand as human as mine? Must there not have been a living person all the while in that room? I cannot tell. I cannot do more than state the fact.

Another surprising circumstance: my watch was restored to the table from which it had been so mysteriously withdrawn. But it had stopped at the very moment it was taken, and despite all the skill of the watchmaker, it has never gone since.

Nothing more happened for the rest of the night. Nor, indeed, had I long to wait before the dawn broke. Nor till it was broad daylight did I leave the haunted house. Before I did so, I revisited the little room in which my servant and I had been for a time imprisoned. I had a strong impression that from that room had originated the phenomena which had been experienced in my chamber. And though I entered it now in the clear day, with the sun peering through the filmy window, I still felt the creep of horror which I had first experienced there the night before. I could not, indeed, bear to stay more than half a minute within those walls.

I descended the stairs, and again I heard the footsteps before me; and when I opened the street door, I thought I could distinguish a very low laugh.

I went at once to Mr. Jones's house. I returned the keys to him, told him that my curiosity was gratified, and related quickly what had passed.

"What on earth can I do with the house?" he said when I had finished.

"I will tell you what I would do. I am convinced from my own feelings that the small unfurnished room at right angles to the door of the bedroom which I occupied, forms a starting point for the influences which haunt the house. I strongly advise you to have the walls opened, the floor removed—indeed, the whole room pulled down."

Mr. Jones appeared to agree to my advice, and about ten days afterwards I received a letter from him saying that he had visited the house and had found the two letters I had described replaced in the drawer from which I had taken them. He had read them with misgivings like my own, and had made a cautious inquiry about the woman to whom they had been written.

It seemed that thirty-six years ago (a year before the date of the letters) she had married, against her family's wishes, an American of very suspicious character. In fact, he was generally believed to have been a pirate. She herself was the daughter of very respectable tradespeople, and had been a nursery governess before her marriage. She had a brother, a widower, who was considered wealthy and who had one child of about six years old. A month after the marriage, the body of this brother was found in the Thames, near London Bridge. There seemed some marks of violence about his throat, but they were not deemed sufficient to warrant any other verdict than that of "found drowned."

The American and his wife took charge of the little boy, the deceased brother having made his sister the guardian of his only child. And in the event of the child's death, the sister inherited. The child died about six months afterwards. It was supposed to have been neglected and ill-treated. The neighbors swore they heard it shriek at night. The surgeon who had examined it after death said that it was emaciated as if from lack of food, and the body was covered with bruises.

It seemed that one winter night the child had tried to escape . . . crept out into the backyard . . . tried to scale the wall . . . fell back exhausted, and had been found next morning on the stones, dying. But though there was some evidence of cruelty, there was none of murder. And the aunt and her husband had sought to excuse the cruelty by declaring the stubbornness and perversity of the child, who was said to be half-witted.

Be that as it may, at the orphan's death, his aunt inherited her brother's fortune. Before the first wedded year was out, the American left England suddenly, and never returned. He obtained a cruising vessel, which was lost in the Atlantic two years afterwards. The widow was left in wealth, but reverses of various kinds had befallen her and her money was lost. Then she entered service, sinking lower and lower, from housekeeper down to maid-of-all-work—never long retaining a place. And so she had dropped into the workhouse, from which Mr. Jones had taken her, to be placed in charge of the very house which she had rented as mistress in the first year of her wedded life.

Mr. Jones added that he had passed an hour alone in the unfurnished room which I had urged him to destroy, and that his impressions of dread while there were so great, though he had neither heard nor seen anything, that he was eager to have the walls bared and the floor removed as I had suggested. He had engaged men for the work, and would commence any day I named.

The date was fixed. We went into the dreary little room,

took up the skirting boards, and then the floors. Under the rafters, covered with rubbish, we found a trap-door, quite large enough for a man to get through. It was closely nailed down with clamps and rivets of iron. On removing these, we descended into a room below, the existence of which had never been suspected. In this room there had been a window and a flue, but they had been bricked over evidently for many years. With the help of candles we examined the place. There was some mouldering furniture, all in the fashion of about eighty years ago. In a chest of drawers against the wall we found, half rotted away, old-fashioned articles of a man's dress, such as might have been worn eighty or a hundred years ago by a gentleman of some rank—costly steel buckles and buttons, a handsome sword. In a waistcoat which had once been rich with gold lace, but which was now blackened and foul with damp, we found five guineas, a few silver coins, and a ticket, probably for some place of entertainment long since passed away. But our main discovery was in a kind of iron safe fixed to the wall, the lock of which took much trouble to pick.

In this safe were three shelves and two small drawers. Ranged on the shelves were several small crystal bottles, sealed air-tight. They contained colorless liquids, which we discovered to be non-poisonous. There were also some very curious glass tubes and a small pointed rod of iron, with a large lump of rock-crystal and another of amber; also a magnet of great power.

In one of the drawers we found a miniature portrait set in gold, and retaining the freshness of its colors most remarkably, considering the length of time it had probably been there. The portrait was of a man who was perhaps forty-seven or forty-eight.

It was a remarkable face—a most impressive face. If you could imagine a serpent transformed into a man, you would have a better idea of that face than long descriptions can convey: the width and flatness—the tapering elegance and strength of the deadly jaw—the long, large, terrible eye, glittering and green as an emerald.

Mechanically, I turned round the miniature to examine the back of it, and on the back was engraved the date 1765. Examining still more minutely, I detected a spring; this, on being pressed, opened the back of the miniature as a lid. Inside the lid was engraved, "Marianna to thee— be faithful in life and in death to ——." Here follows a name that I will not mention, but it was familiar to me. I had heard it spoken of by old men in my childhood as the name borne by a criminal who had made a great sensation in London for a year or so, and had fled the country on the charge of a double murder within his own house: that of his mistress and his rival.

We found no difficulty in opening the first drawer within the iron safe; we found great difficulty in opening the second: it was not locked, but it resisted all efforts, till we inserted the edge of a chisel. Inside, on a small thin book, was placed a crystal saucer: this saucer was filled with a clear liquid, on which floated a kind of compass with a needle shifting rapidly round. But instead of the usual points of a compass were seven strange characters, like those used by astrologers to denote the planets.

A peculiar, but not strong nor displeasing odor came

176

from this drawer, which was lined with hazelwood. Whatever the cause of this odor, it affected the nerves. We all felt it, even the two workmen who were in the room—a creeping, tingling sensation from the tips of the fingers to the roots of the hair. Impatient to examine the book, I removed the saucer. As I did so the needle of the compass went round and round with great swiftness, and I felt a shock that ran through my whole body, so that I dropped the saucer on the floor. The liquid was spilt; the saucer was broken; the compass rolled to the end of the room. And at that moment the walls shook to and fro, as if a giant had swayed and rocked them.

The two workmen were so frightened that they ran up the ladder by which we had descended from the trap-door; but seeing that nothing more happened, they returned.

Meanwhile I had opened the book. It was bound in plain red leather, with a silver clasp. It contained but one sheet of thick vellum, and on that sheet were inscribed words in old monkish Latin, which literally translated were: "On all that it can reach within these walls—living or dead—as moves the needle, so work my will! Accursed be the house, and restless be the dwellers therein."

We found no more. Mr. Jones burnt the book and razed to the foundations the part of the building containing the secret room with the chamber over it. He had then the courage to inhabit the house himself, and a quieter, better-conditioned house could not be found in all London.

8109

SC
HAU

A Haunt of ghosts

$12.70

DATE			
FEB 12 '89			
MAR 23 '89			
APR 6 '89			
NOV 18 '90			

Edwards Knox School Library
Russell, New York

© THE BAKER & TAYLOR CO.